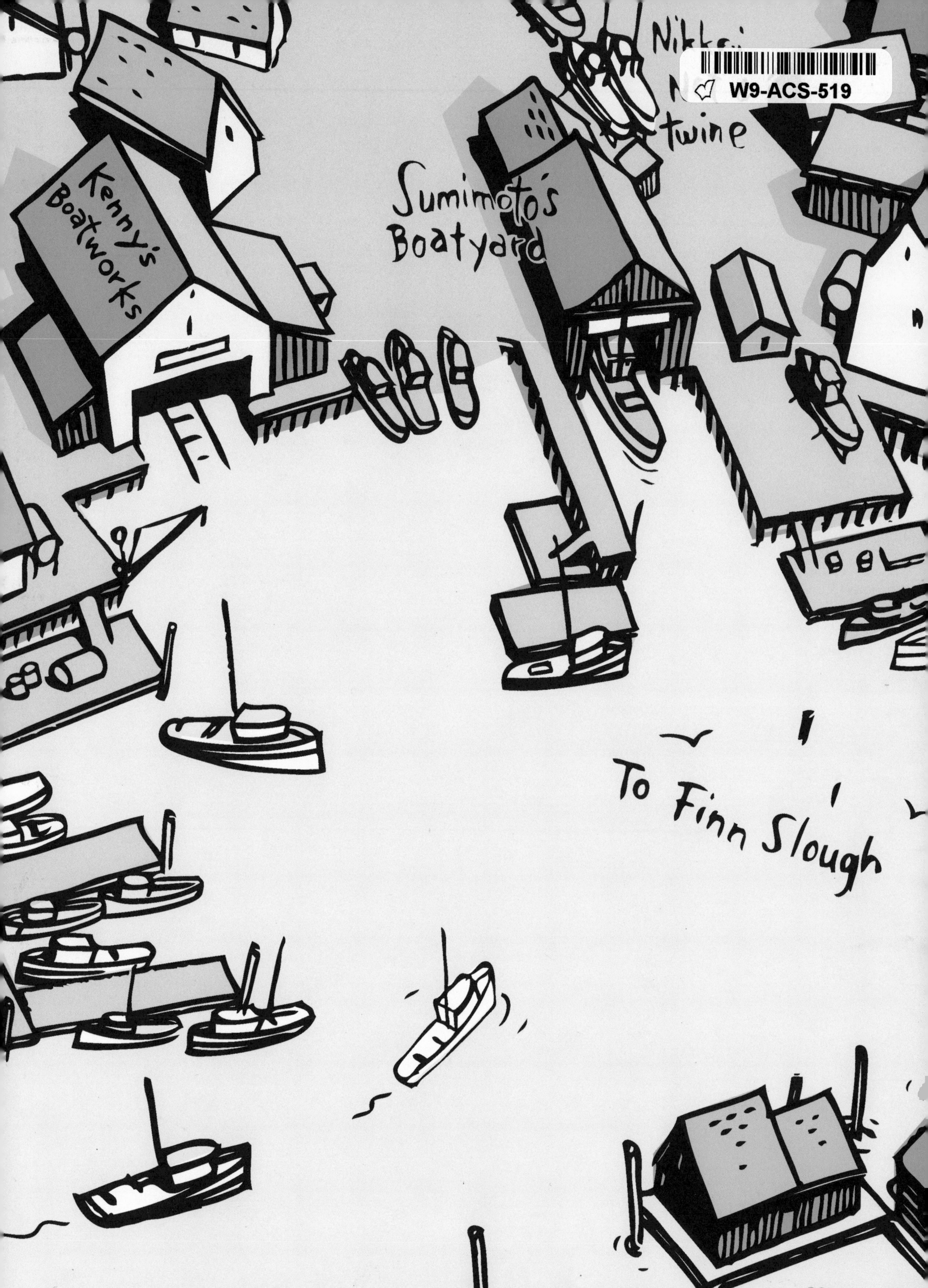
Kenny's Boatworks
Sumimoto's Boatyard
twine
To Finn Slough

Gubby Builds a Boat

by Gary Kent
illustrated by Kim La Fave

Harbour Publishing

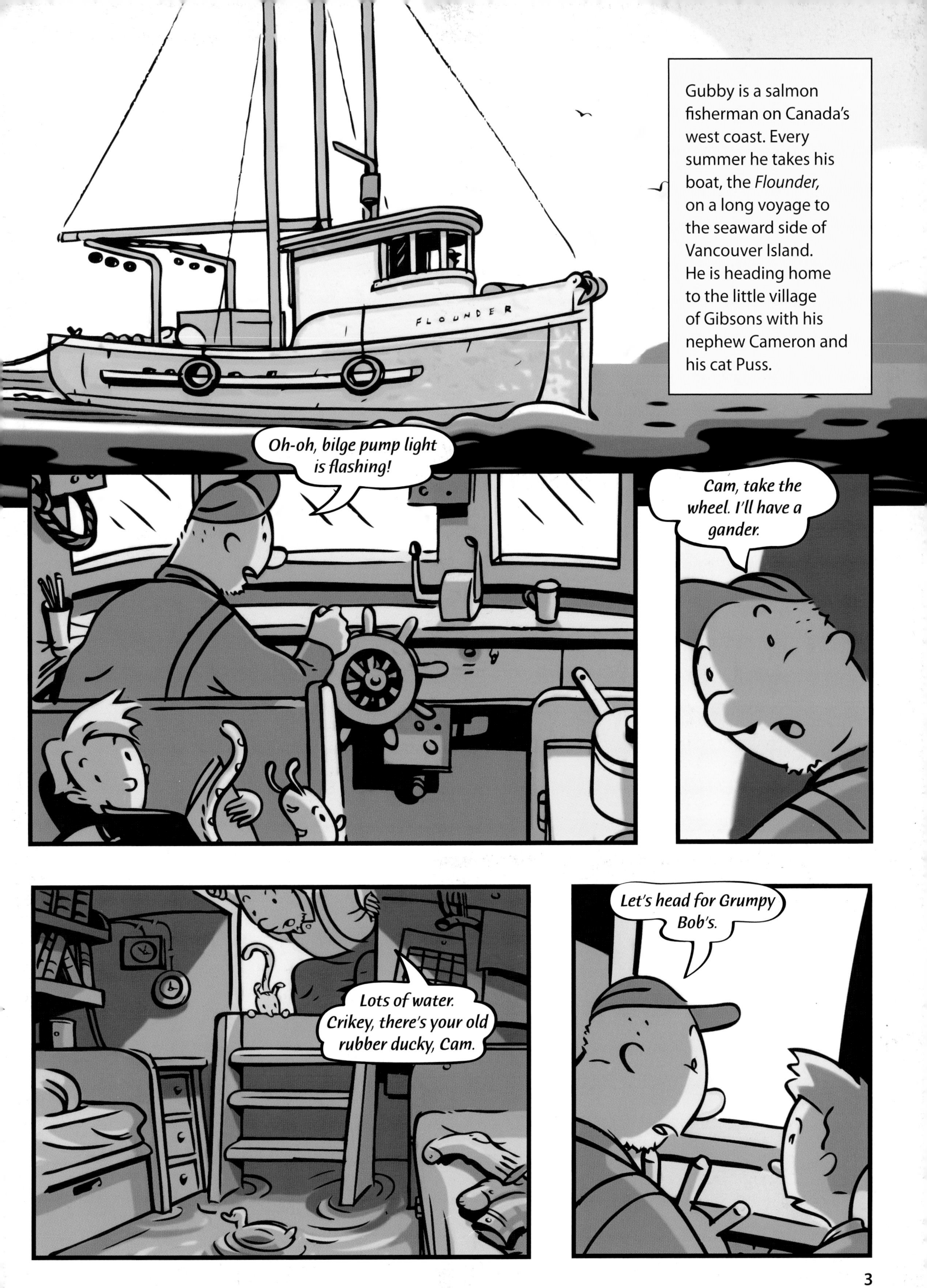
Gubby is a salmon fisherman on Canada's west coast. Every summer he takes his boat, the *Flounder,* on a long voyage to the seaward side of Vancouver Island. He is heading home to the little village of Gibsons with his nephew Cameron and his cat Puss.
FLOUNDER
Oh-oh, bilge pump light is flashing!
Cam, take the wheel. I'll have a gander.
Lots of water. Crikey, there's your old rubber ducky, Cam.
Let's head for Grumpy Bob's.

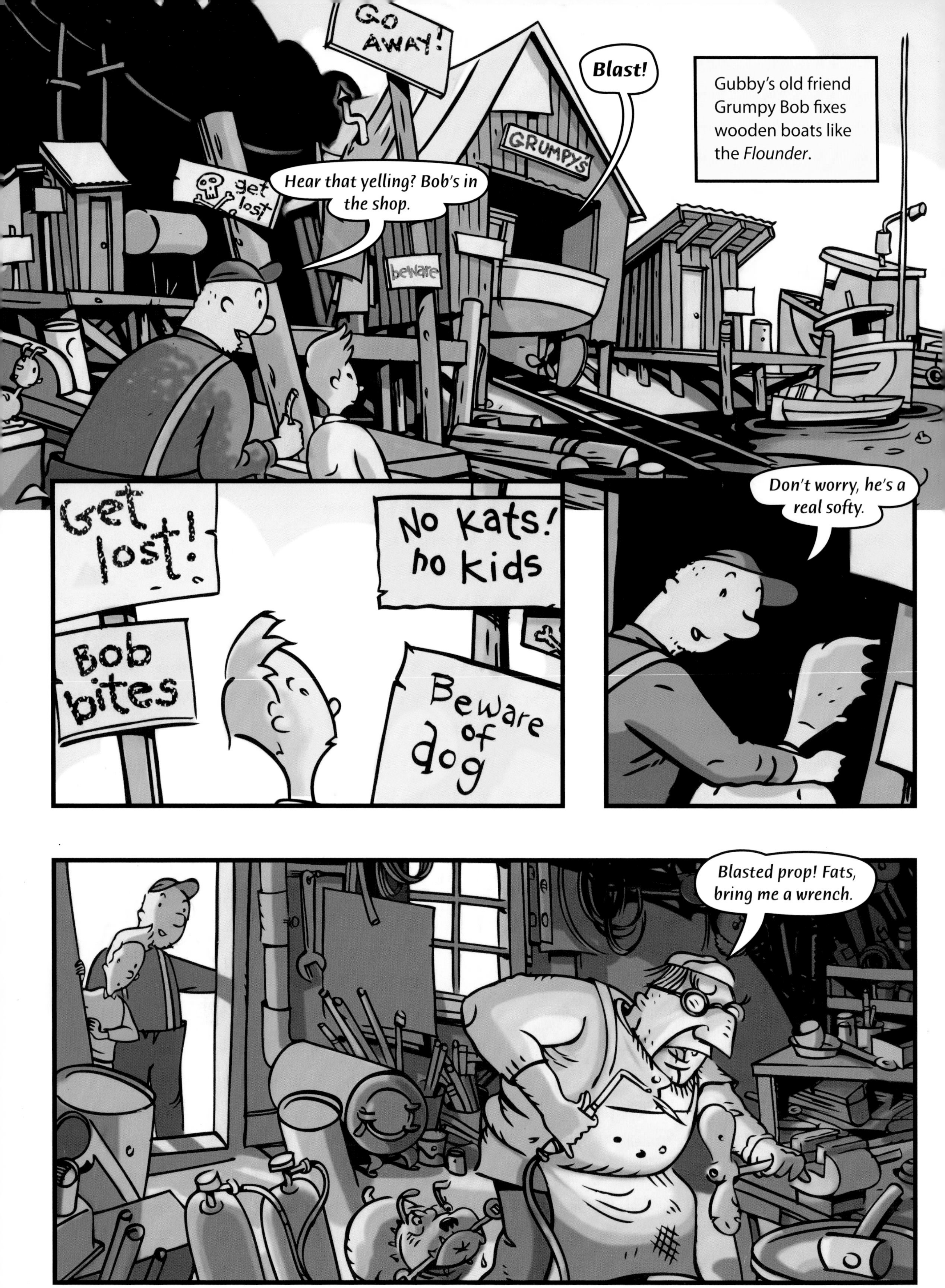
GO AWAY!
Blast!
Gubby's old friend Grumpy Bob fixes wooden boats like the *Flounder*.
GRUMPY'S
get lost
Hear that yelling? Bob's in the shop.
beware
Get lost!
No kats! no kids
Bob bites
Beware of dog
Don't worry, he's a real softy.
Blasted prop! Fats, bring me a wrench.

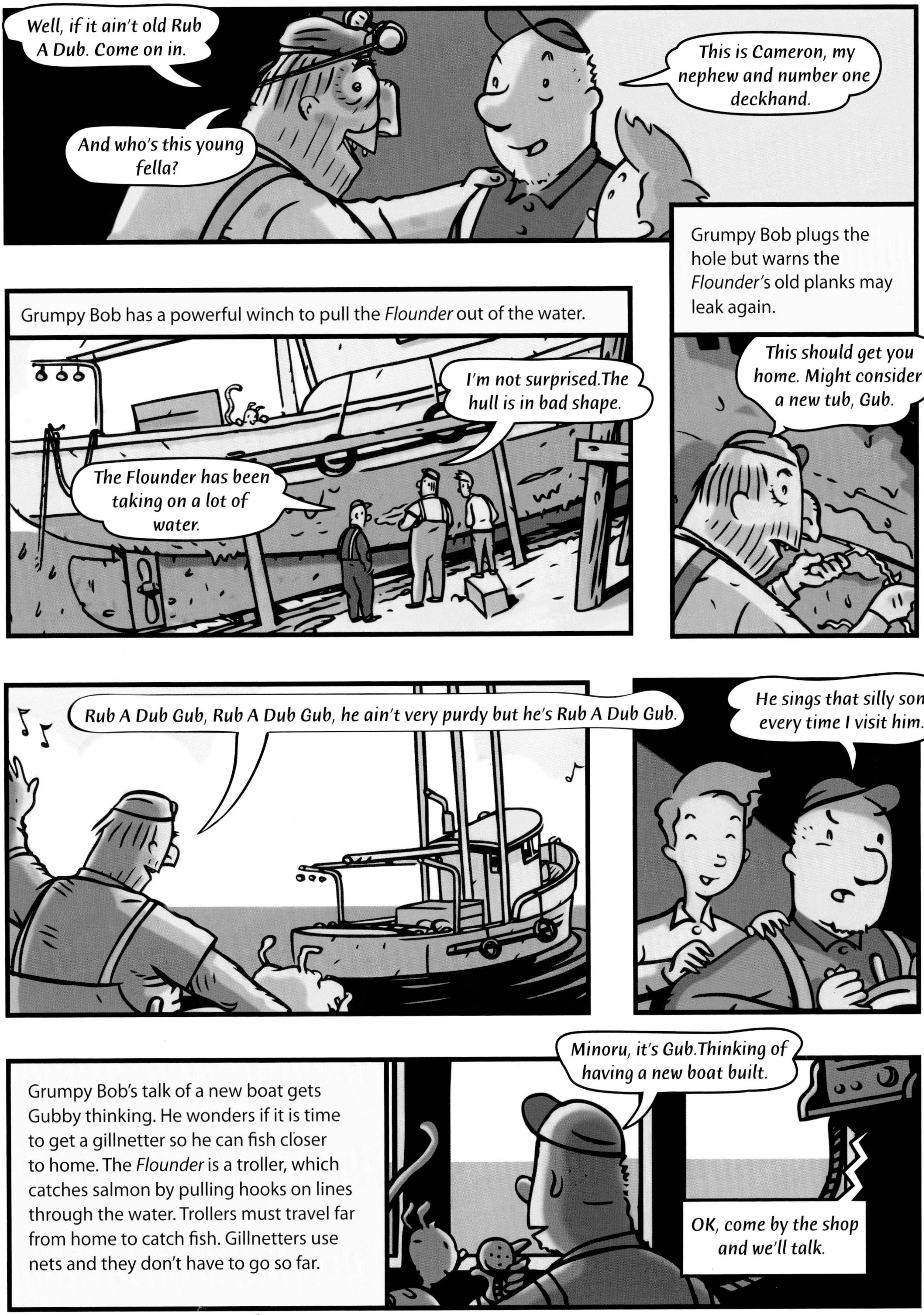

Well, if it ain't old Rub A Dub. Come on in.
And who's this young fella?
This is Cameron, my nephew and number one deckhand.
Grumpy Bob has a powerful winch to pull the *Flounder* out of the water.
The Flounder has been taking on a lot of water.
I'm not surprised.The hull is in bad shape.
Grumpy Bob plugs the hole but warns the *Flounder's* old planks may leak again.
This should get you home. Might consider a new tub, Gub.
Rub A Dub Gub, Rub A Dub Gub, he ain't very purdy but he's Rub A Dub Gub.
He sings that silly song every time I visit him.
Grumpy Bob's talk of a new boat gets Gubby thinking. He wonders if it is time to get a gillnetter so he can fish closer to home. The *Flounder* is a troller, which catches salmon by pulling hooks on lines through the water. Trollers must travel far from home to catch fish. Gillnetters use nets and they don't have to go so far.
Minoru, it's Gub.Thinking of having a new boat built.
OK, come by the shop and we'll talk.

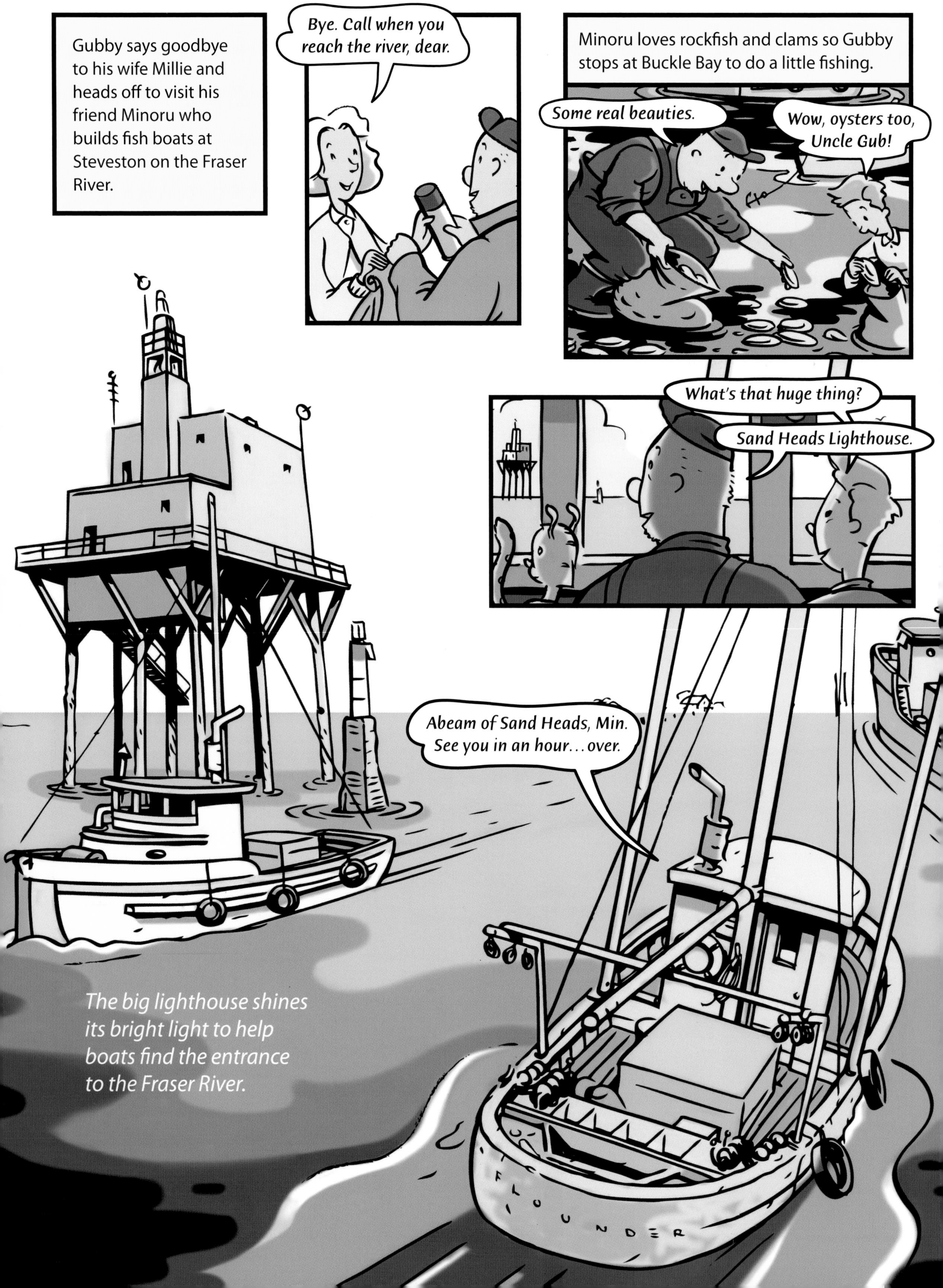
Gubby says goodbye to his wife Millie and heads off to visit his friend Minoru who builds fish boats at Steveston on the Fraser River.
Bye. Call when you reach the river, dear.
Minoru loves rockfish and clams so Gubby stops at Buckle Bay to do a little fishing.
Some real beauties.
Wow, oysters too, Uncle Gub!
What's that huge thing?
Sand Heads Lighthouse.
Abeam of Sand Heads, Min. See you in an hour...over.
The big lighthouse shines its bright light to help boats find the entrance to the Fraser River.
FLOUNDER

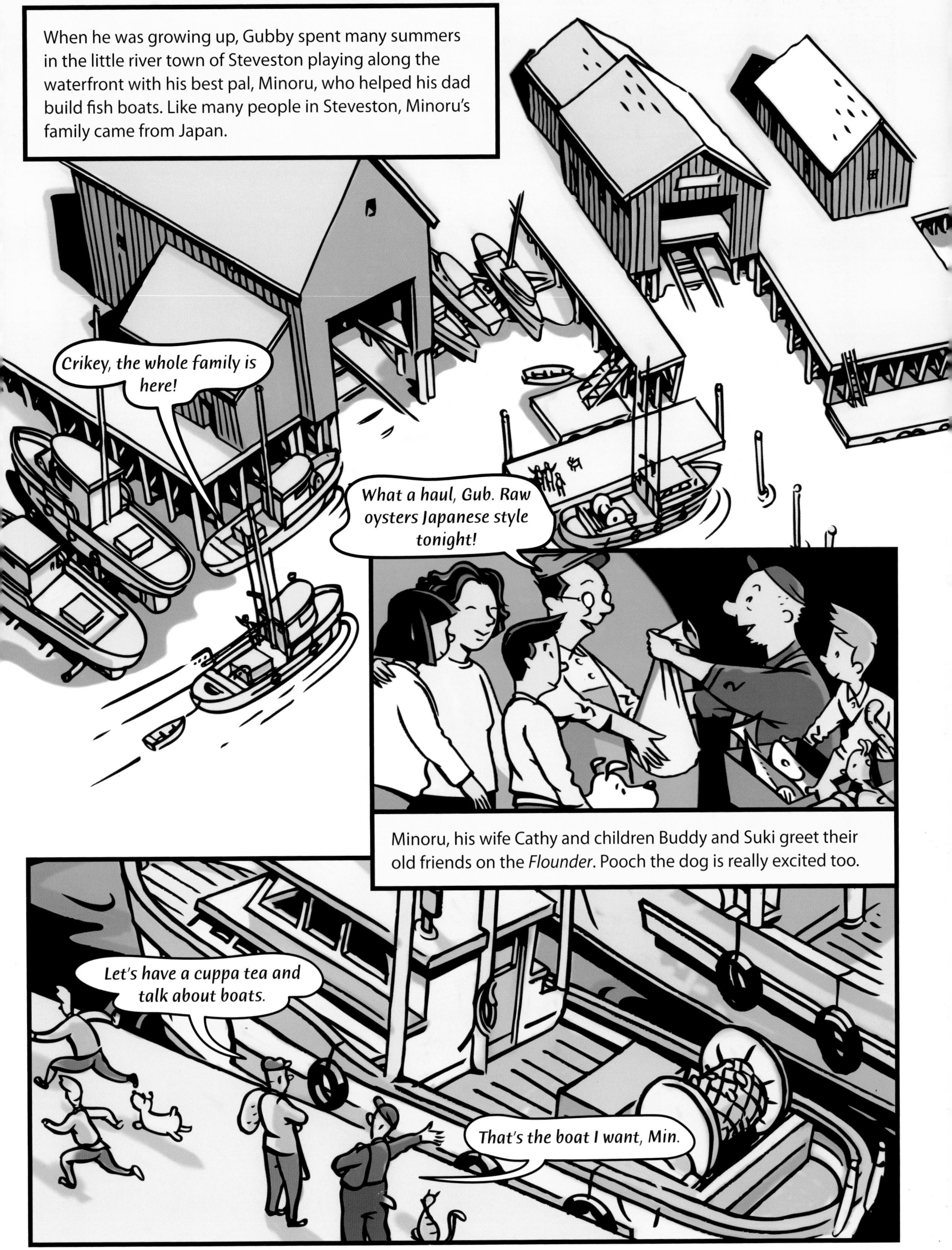
When he was growing up, Gubby spent many summers in the little river town of Steveston playing along the waterfront with his best pal, Minoru, who helped his dad build fish boats. Like many people in Steveston, Minoru's family came from Japan.
Crikey, the whole family is here!
What a haul, Gub. Raw oysters Japanese style tonight!
Minoru, his wife Cathy and children Buddy and Suki greet their old friends on the *Flounder*. Pooch the dog is really excited too.
Let's have a cuppa tea and talk about boats.
That's the boat I want, Min.

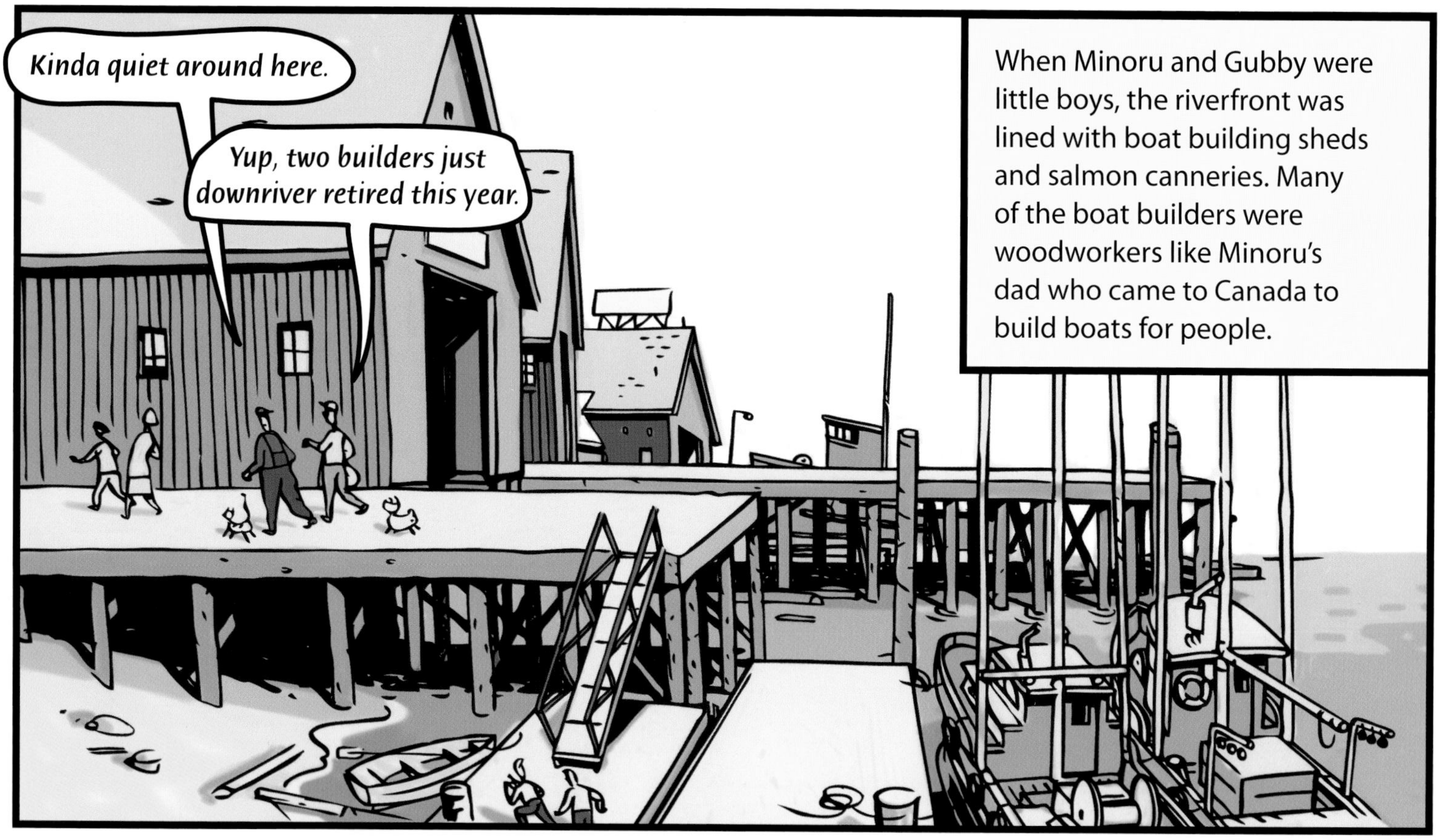
Kinda quiet around here.
Yup, two builders just downriver retired this year.
When Minoru and Gubby were little boys, the riverfront was lined with boat building sheds and salmon canneries. Many of the boat builders were woodworkers like Minoru's dad who came to Canada to build boats for people.

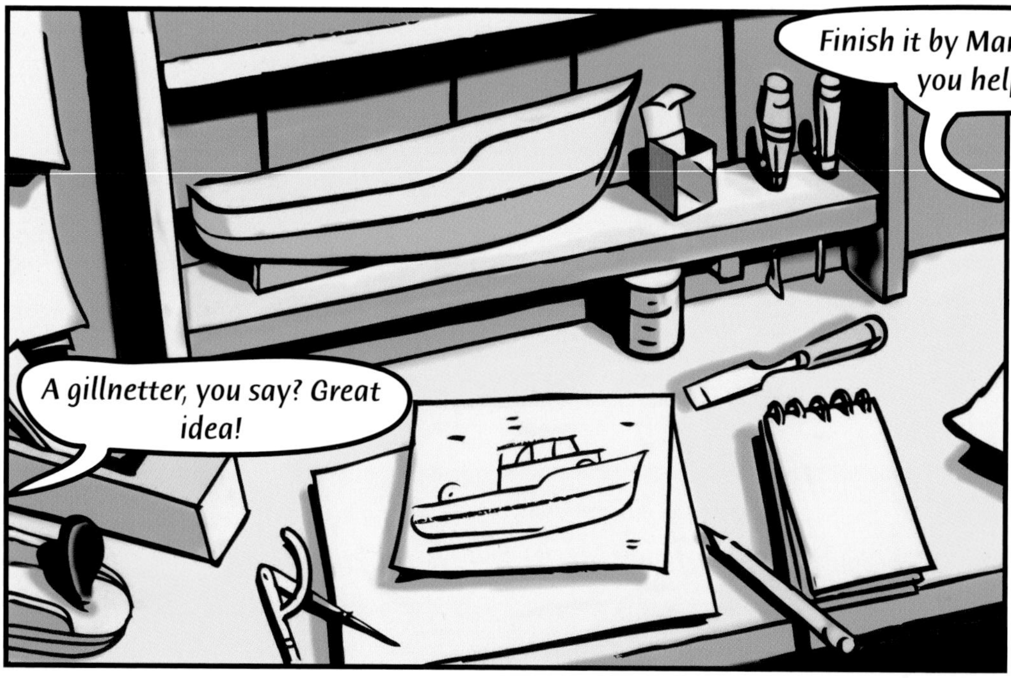
Finish it by March. Cheaper if you help, Gub.
A gillnetter, you say? Great idea!

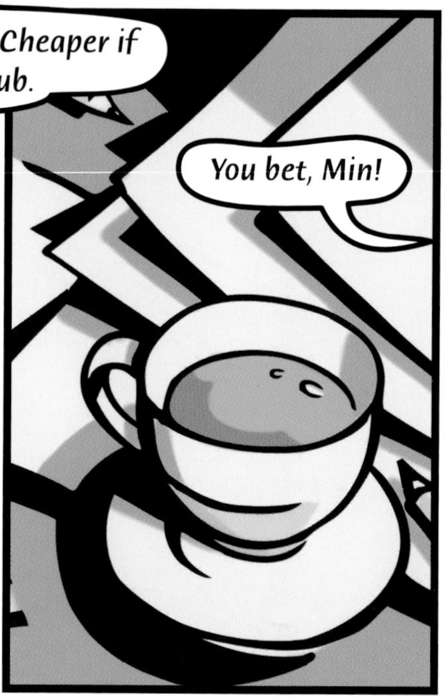
You bet, Min!

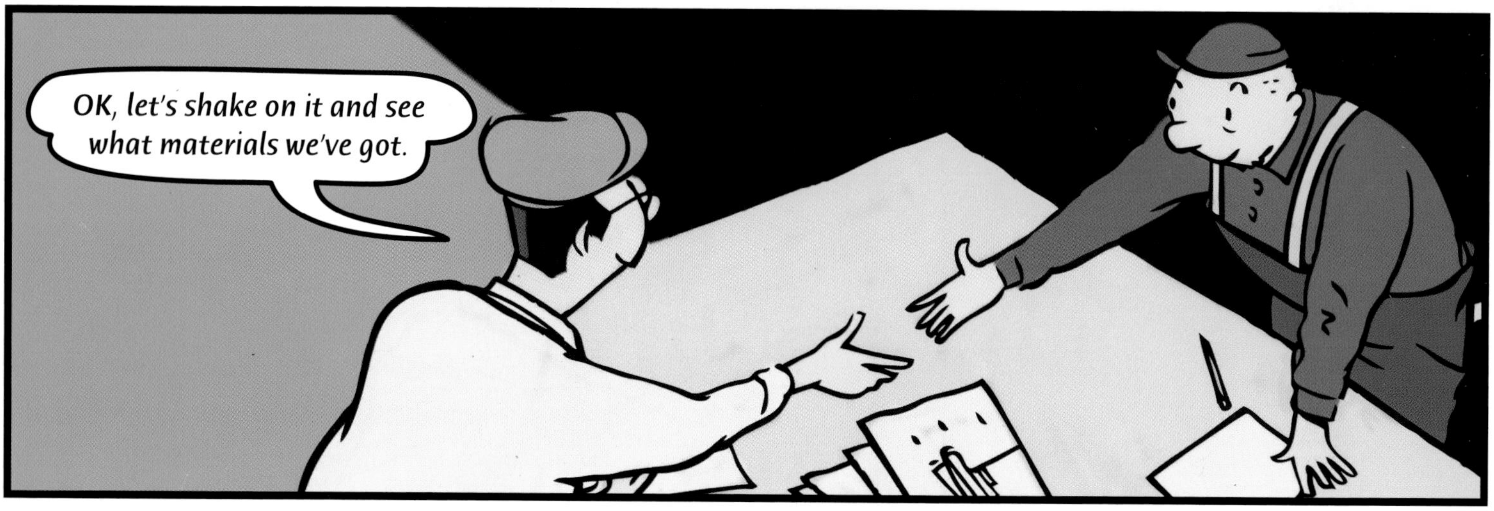
OK, let's shake on it and see what materials we've got.

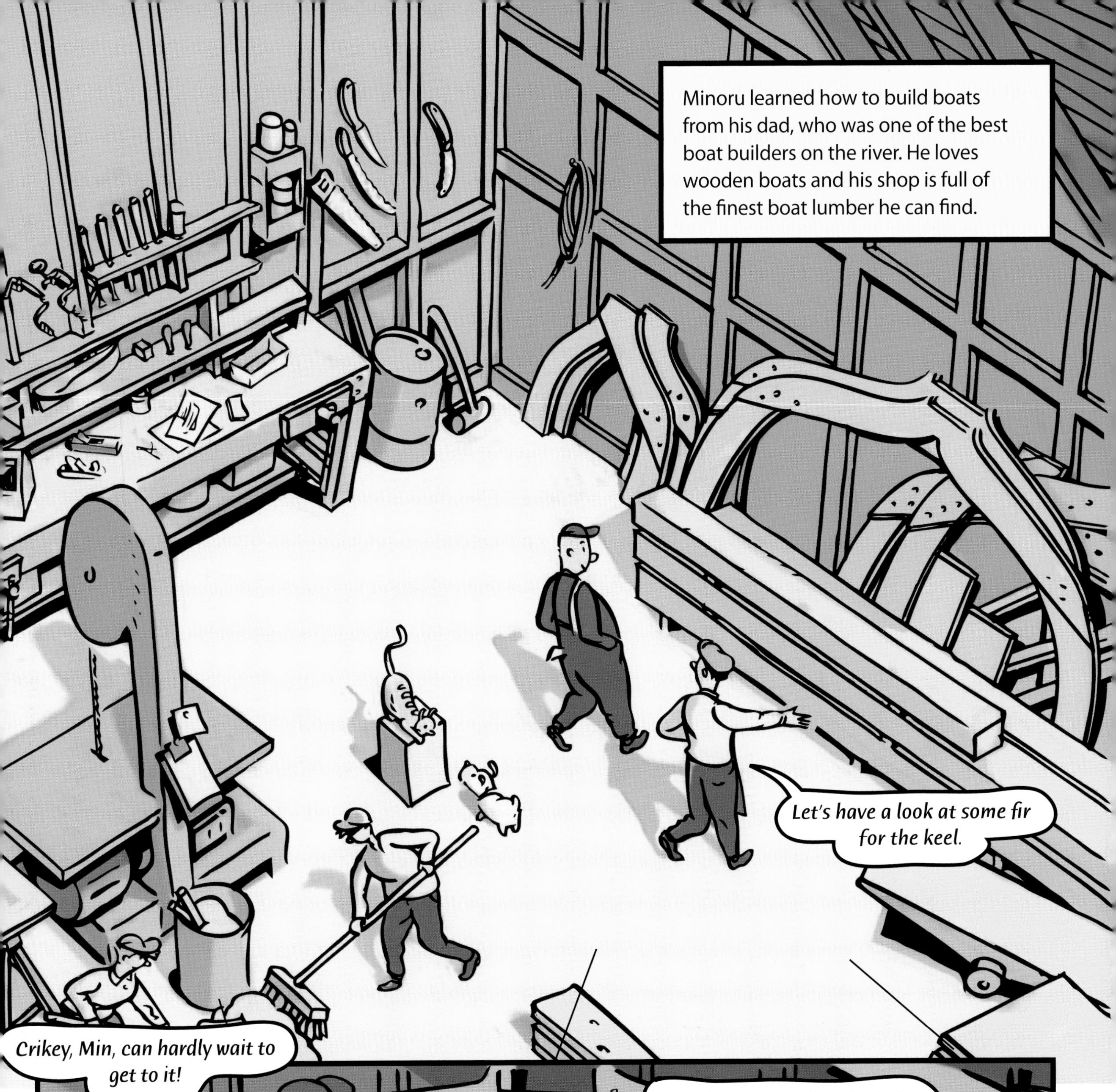
Minoru learned how to build boats from his dad, who was one of the best boat builders on the river. He loves wooden boats and his shop is full of the finest boat lumber he can find.
Let's have a look at some fir for the keel.

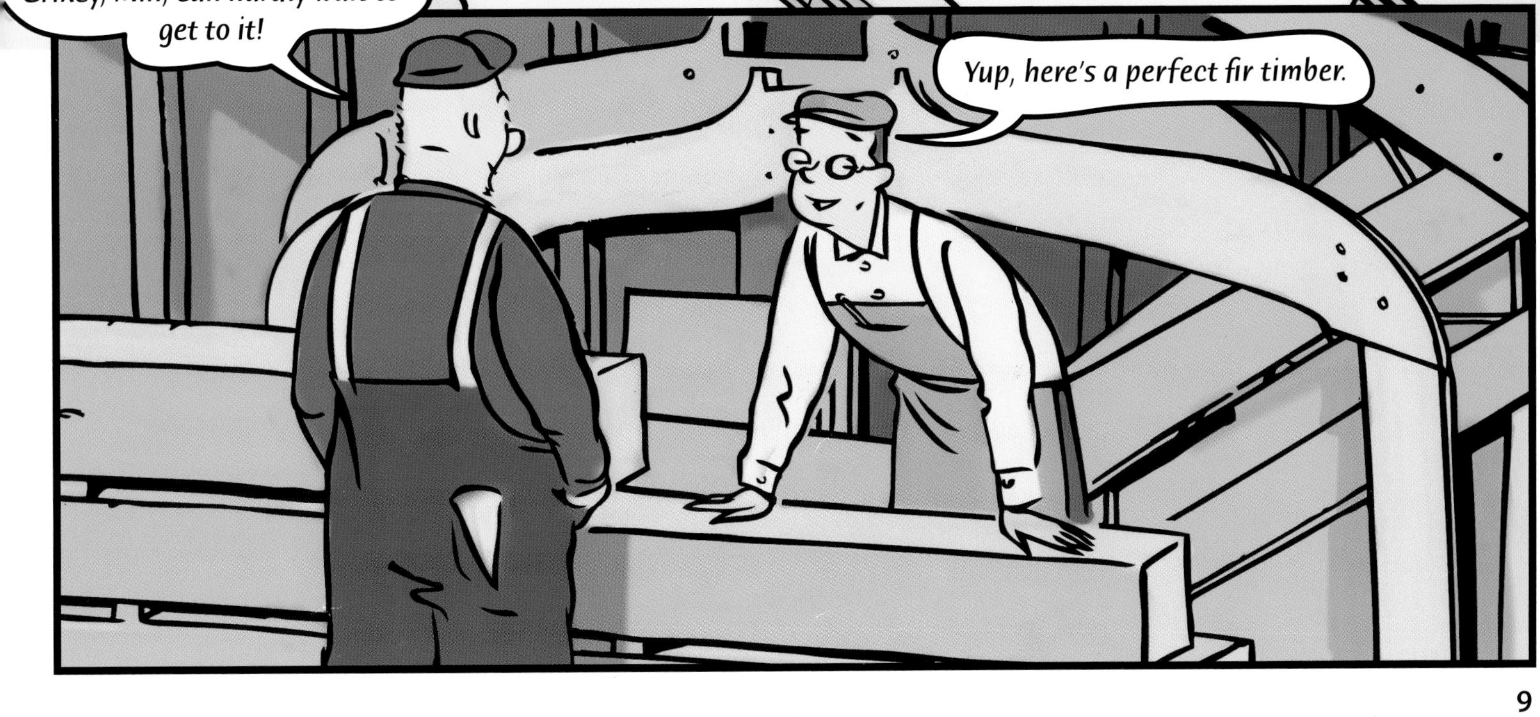
Crikey, Min, can hardly wait to get to it!
Yup, here's a perfect fir timber.

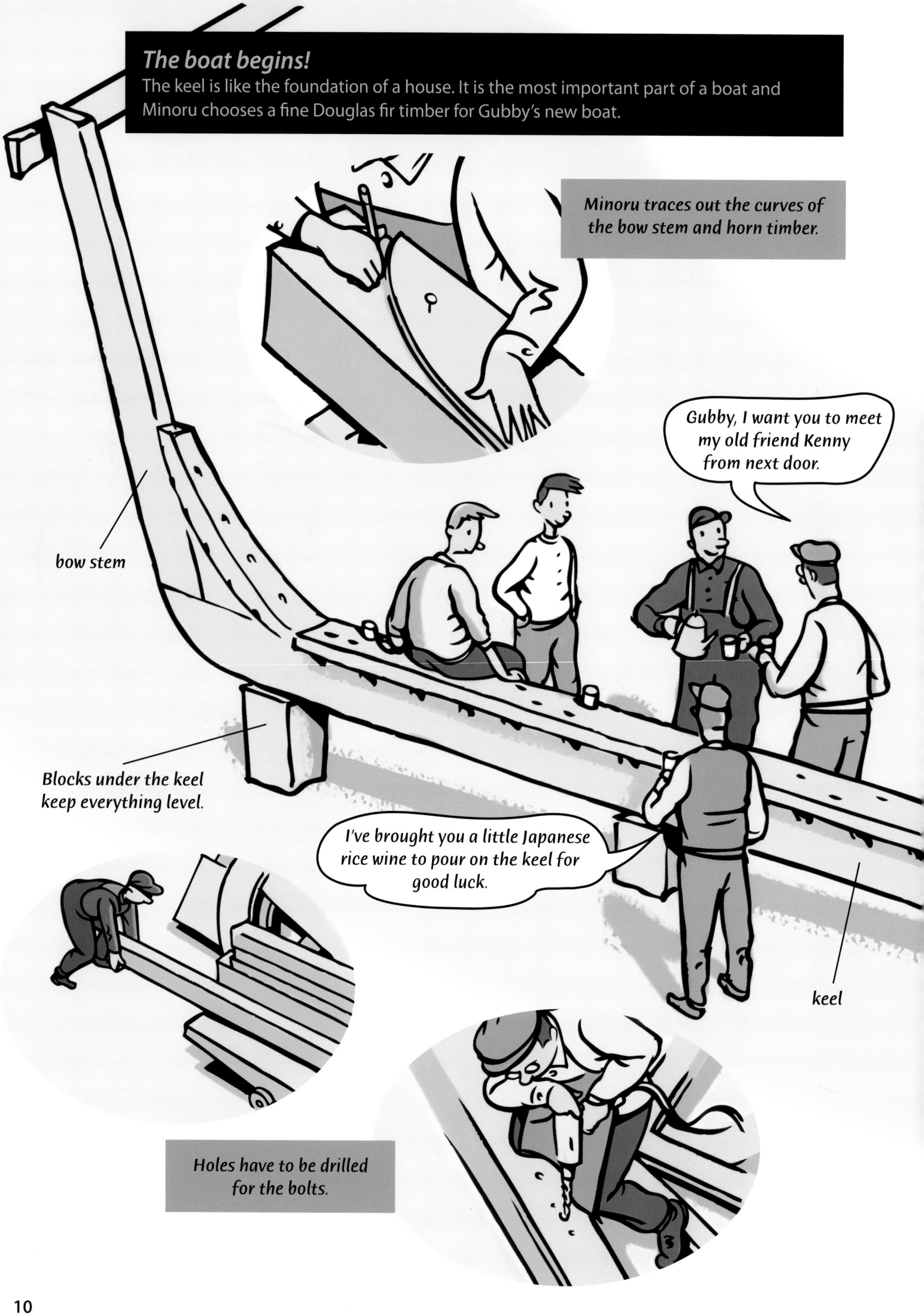
The boat begins!
The keel is like the foundation of a house. It is the most important part of a boat and Minoru chooses a fine Douglas fir timber for Gubby's new boat.
Minoru traces out the curves of the bow stem and horn timber.
Gubby, I want you to meet my old friend Kenny from next door.
bow stem
Blocks under the keel keep everything level.
I've brought you a little Japanese rice wine to pour on the keel for good luck.
keel
Holes have to be drilled for the bolts.

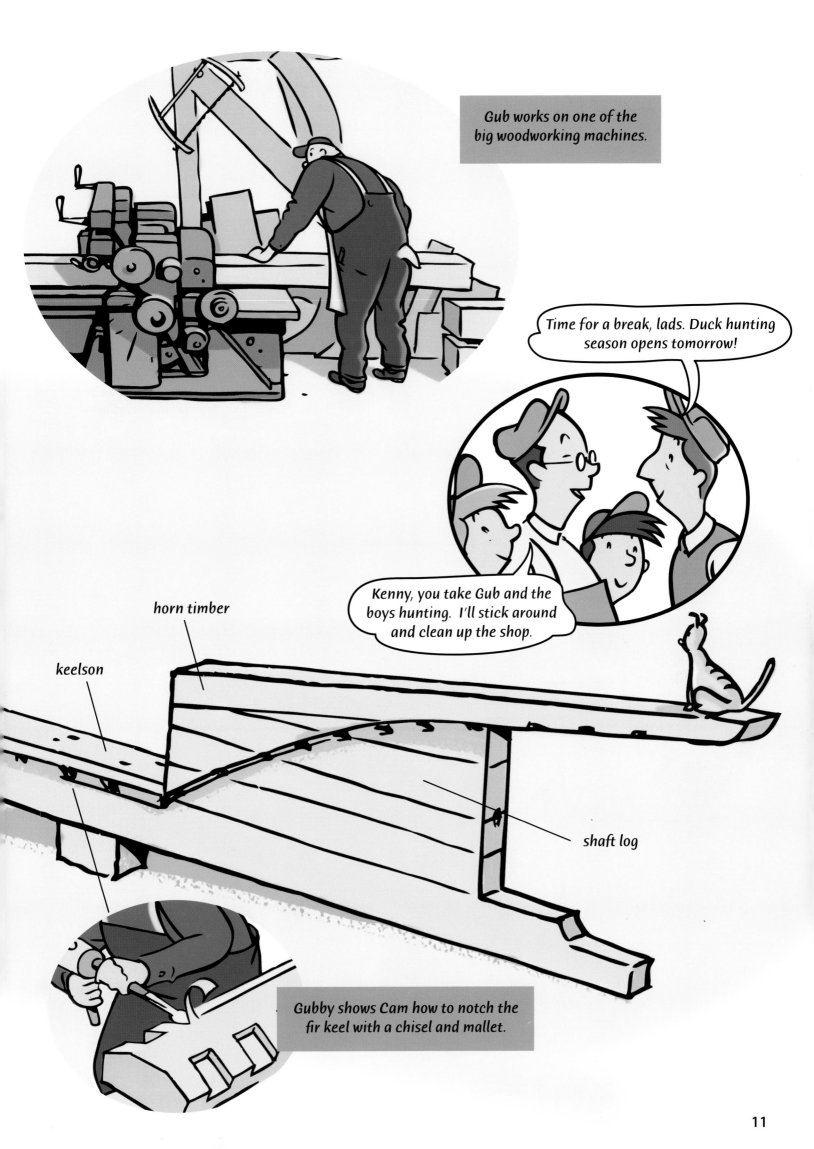

Gub works on one of the big woodworking machines.

Time for a break, lads. Duck hunting season opens tomorrow!

Kenny, you take Gub and the boys hunting. I'll stick around and clean up the shop.

horn timber

keelson

shaft log

Gubby shows Cam how to notch the fir keel with a chisel and mallet.

Pooch wants to go too.

The great hunters of the swamp are off!

A-hunting we will go, a-hunting we will go...

Gub calls the ducks...

Quack, quack!

What in tarnation...!

We're under attack!

You alright, Kenny?

I'm freezing.

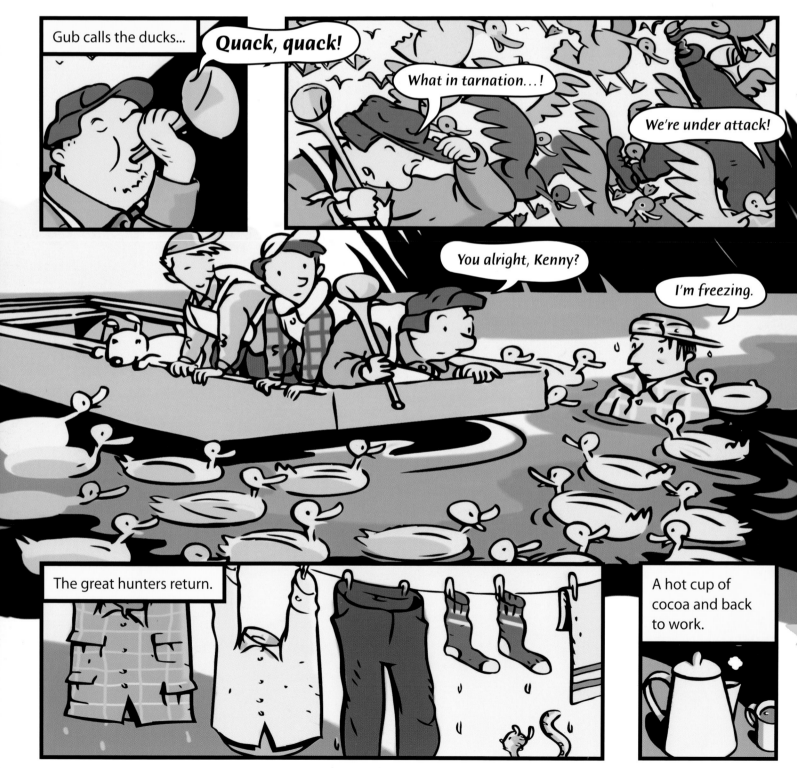

The great hunters return.

A hot cup of cocoa and back to work.

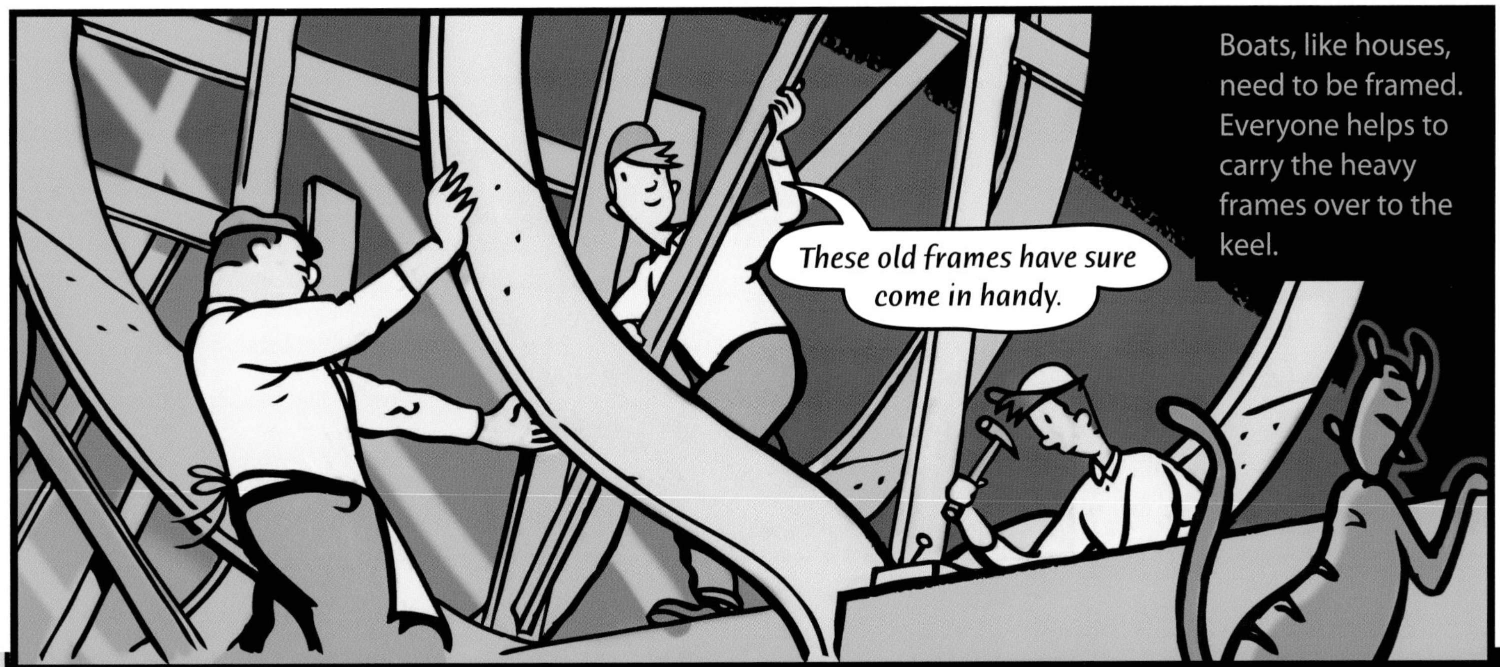
Boats, like houses, need to be framed. Everyone helps to carry the heavy frames over to the keel.
These old frames have sure come in handy.

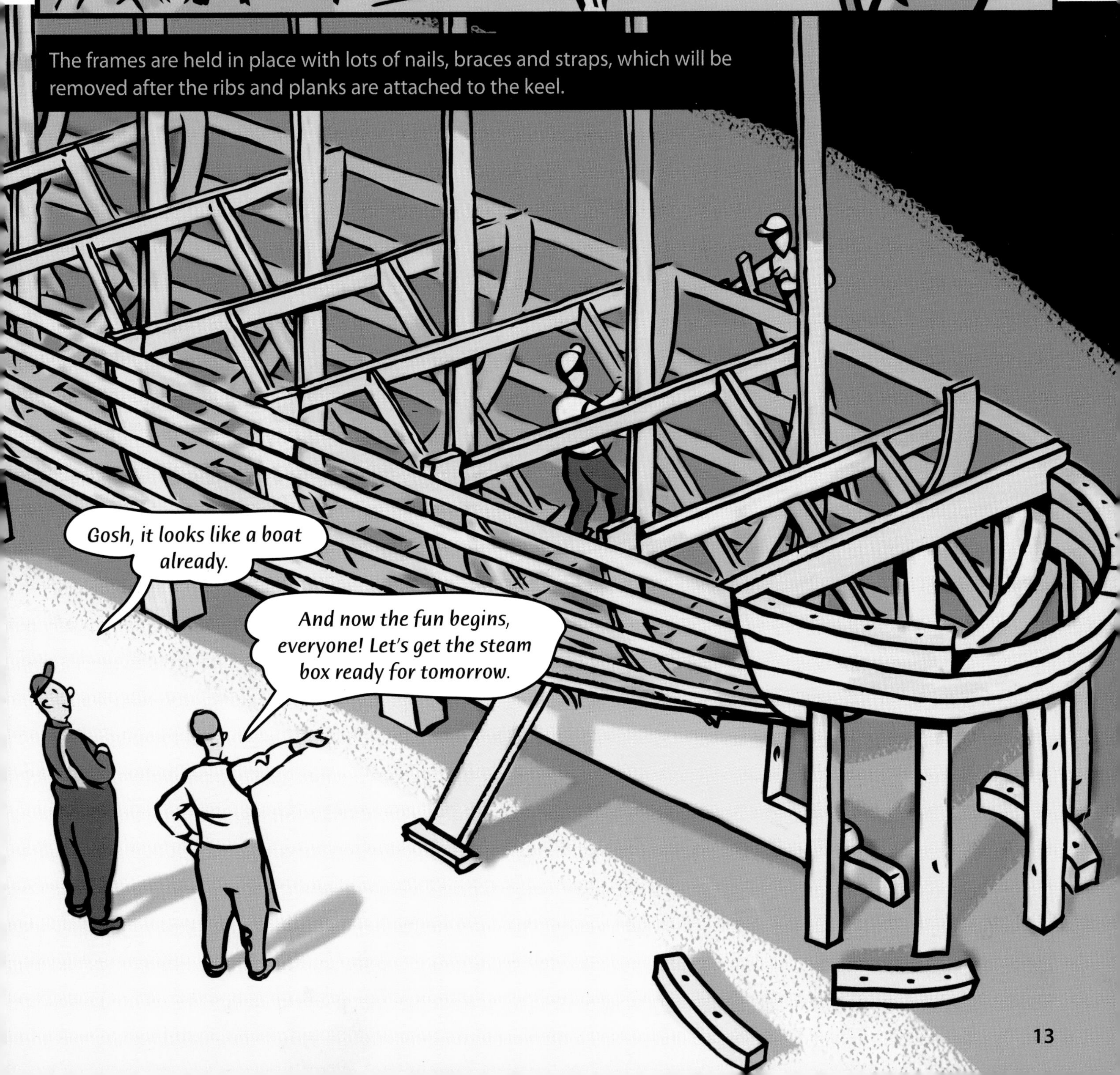
The frames are held in place with lots of nails, braces and straps, which will be removed after the ribs and planks are attached to the keel.
Gosh, it looks like a boat already.
And now the fun begins, everyone! Let's get the steam box ready for tomorrow.

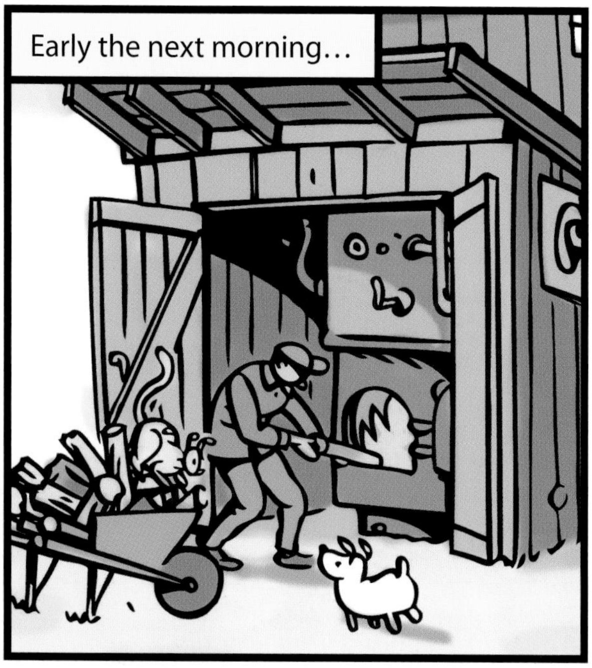
Early the next morning…

Buddy and Cam build a roaring fire in the boiler. Soon the ribs will be softened by clouds of steam.

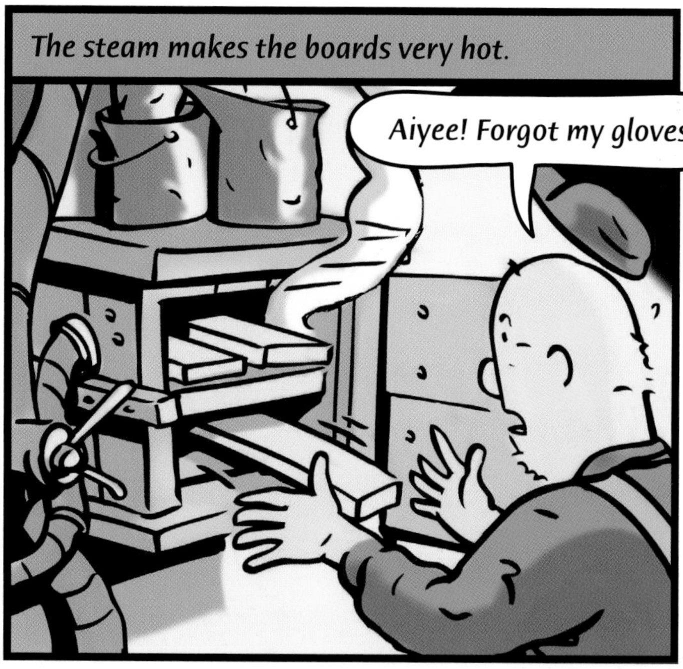
The steam makes the boards very hot.
Aiyee! Forgot my gloves!

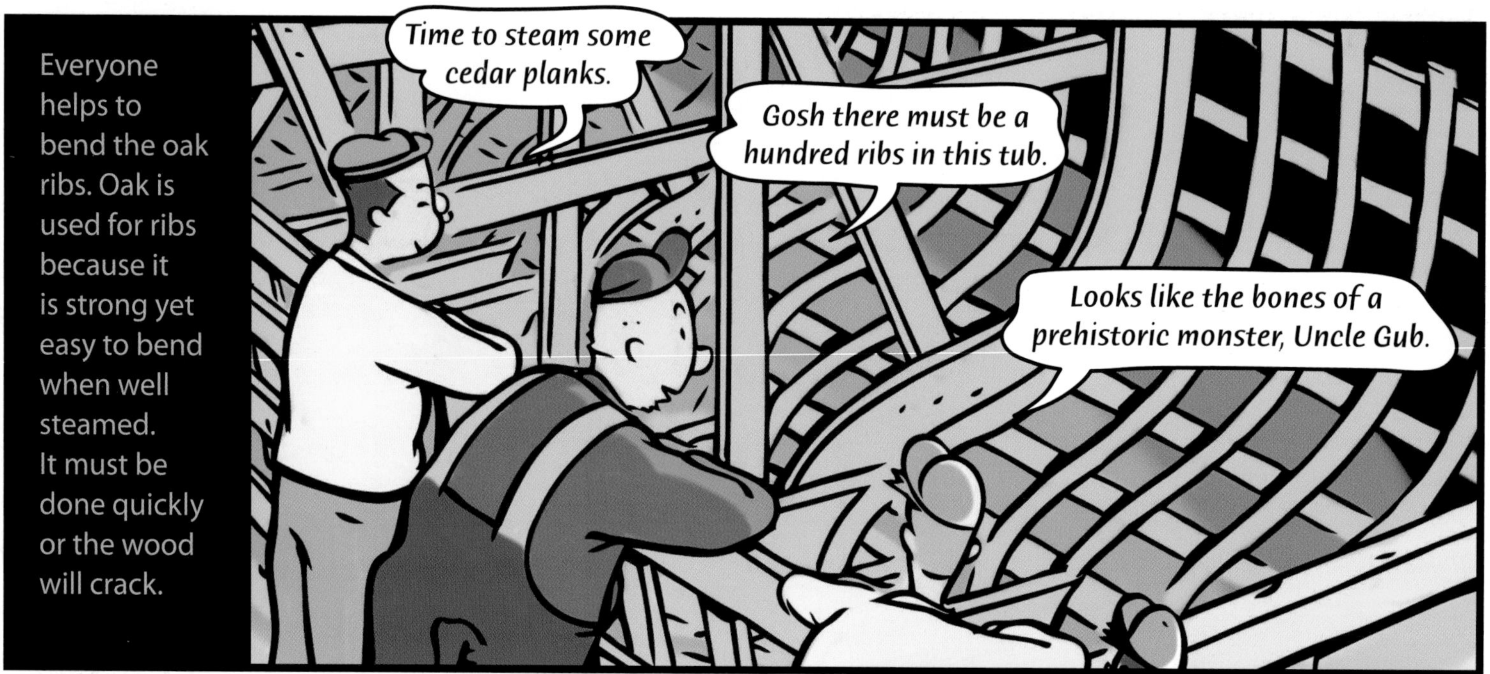
Everyone helps to bend the oak ribs. Oak is used for ribs because it is strong yet easy to bend when well steamed. It must be done quickly or the wood will crack.
Time to steam some cedar planks.
Gosh there must be a hundred ribs in this tub.
Looks like the bones of a prehistoric monster, Uncle Gub.

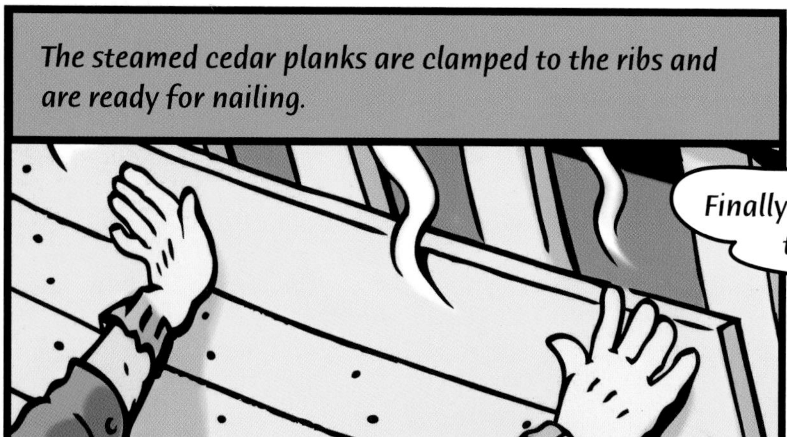
The steamed cedar planks are clamped to the ribs and are ready for nailing.

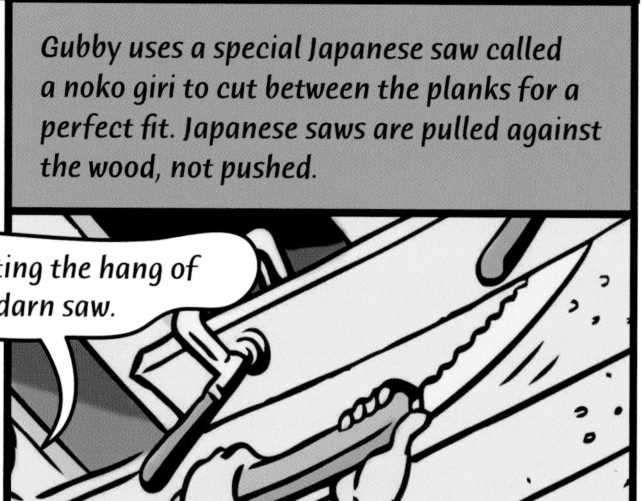
Gubby uses a special Japanese saw called a noko giri to cut between the planks for a perfect fit. Japanese saws are pulled against the wood, not pushed.
Finally getting the hang of this darn saw.

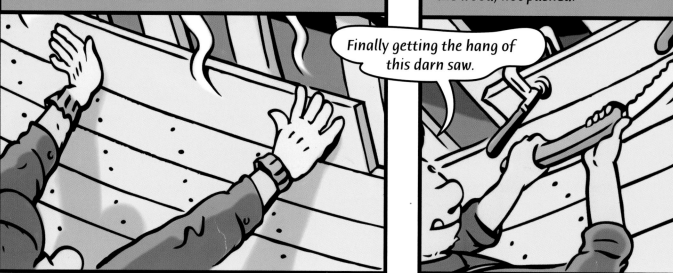

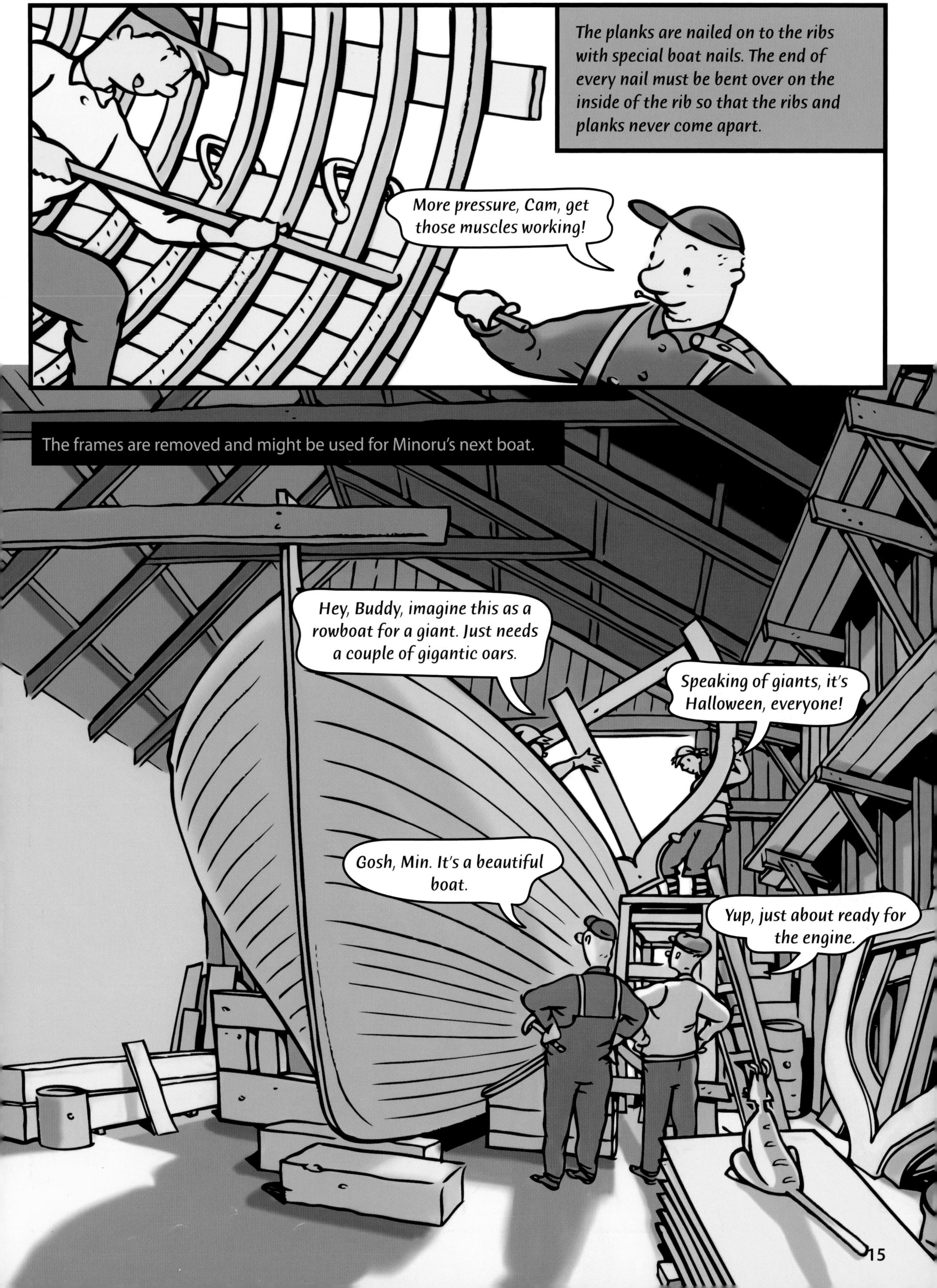
The planks are nailed on to the ribs with special boat nails. The end of every nail must be bent over on the inside of the rib so that the ribs and planks never come apart.
More pressure, Cam, get those muscles working!
The frames are removed and might be used for Minoru's next boat.
Hey, Buddy, imagine this as a rowboat for a giant. Just needs a couple of gigantic oars.
Speaking of giants, it's Halloween, everyone!
Gosh, Min. It's a beautiful boat.
Yup, just about ready for the engine.

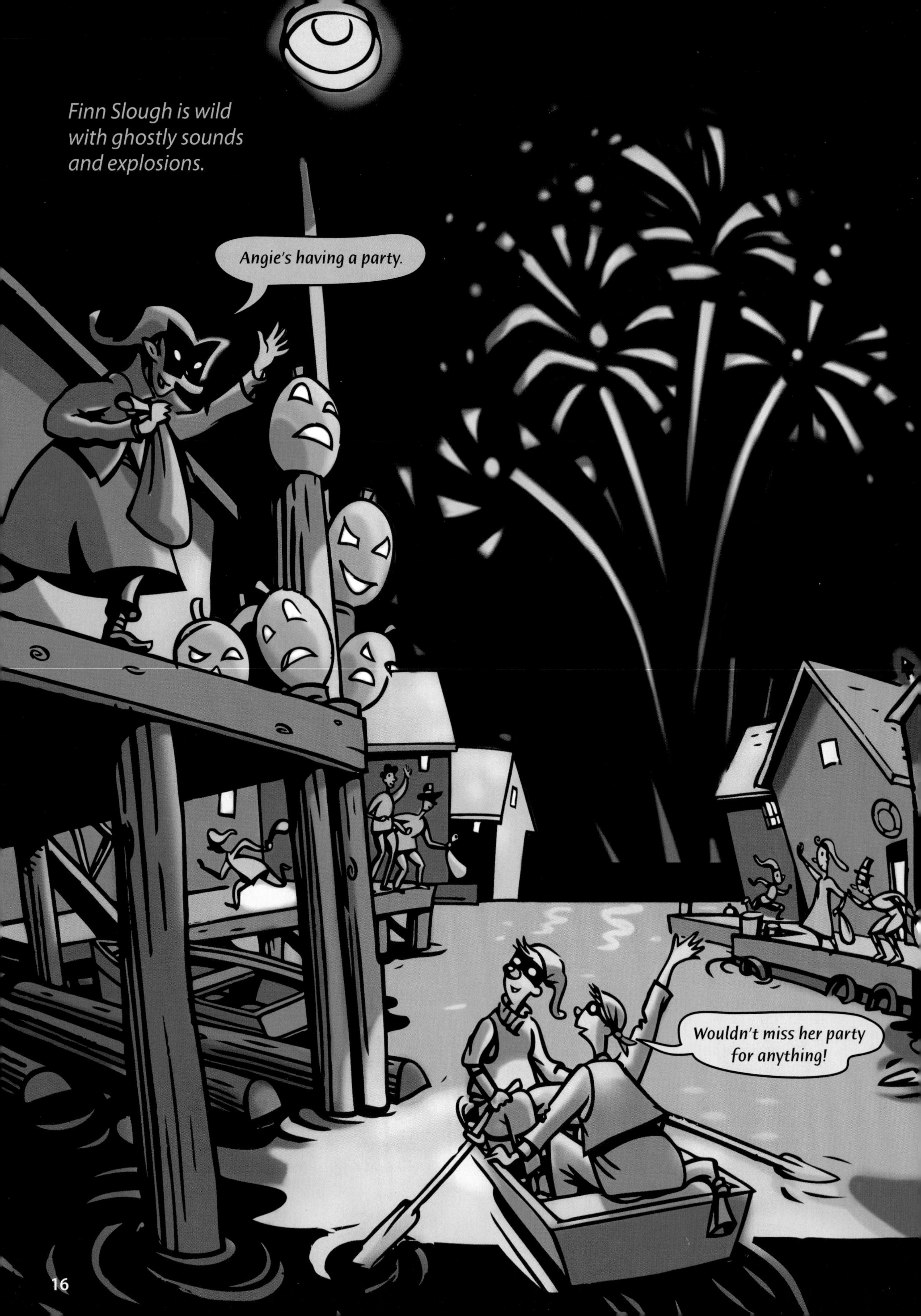
Finn Slough is wild with ghostly sounds and explosions.
Angie's having a party.
Wouldn't miss her party for anything!

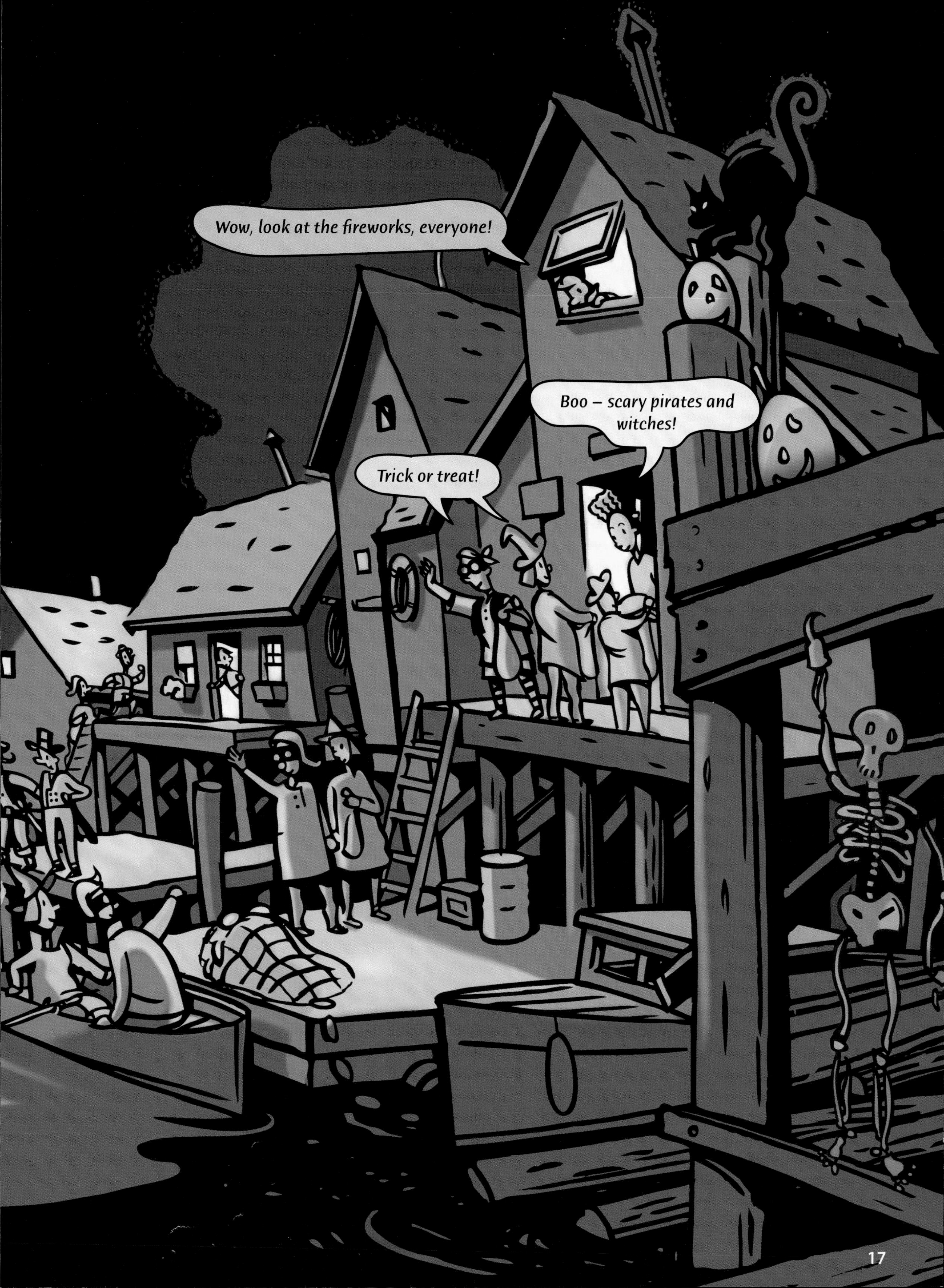
Wow, look at the fireworks, everyone!
Trick or treat!
Boo – scary pirates and witches!

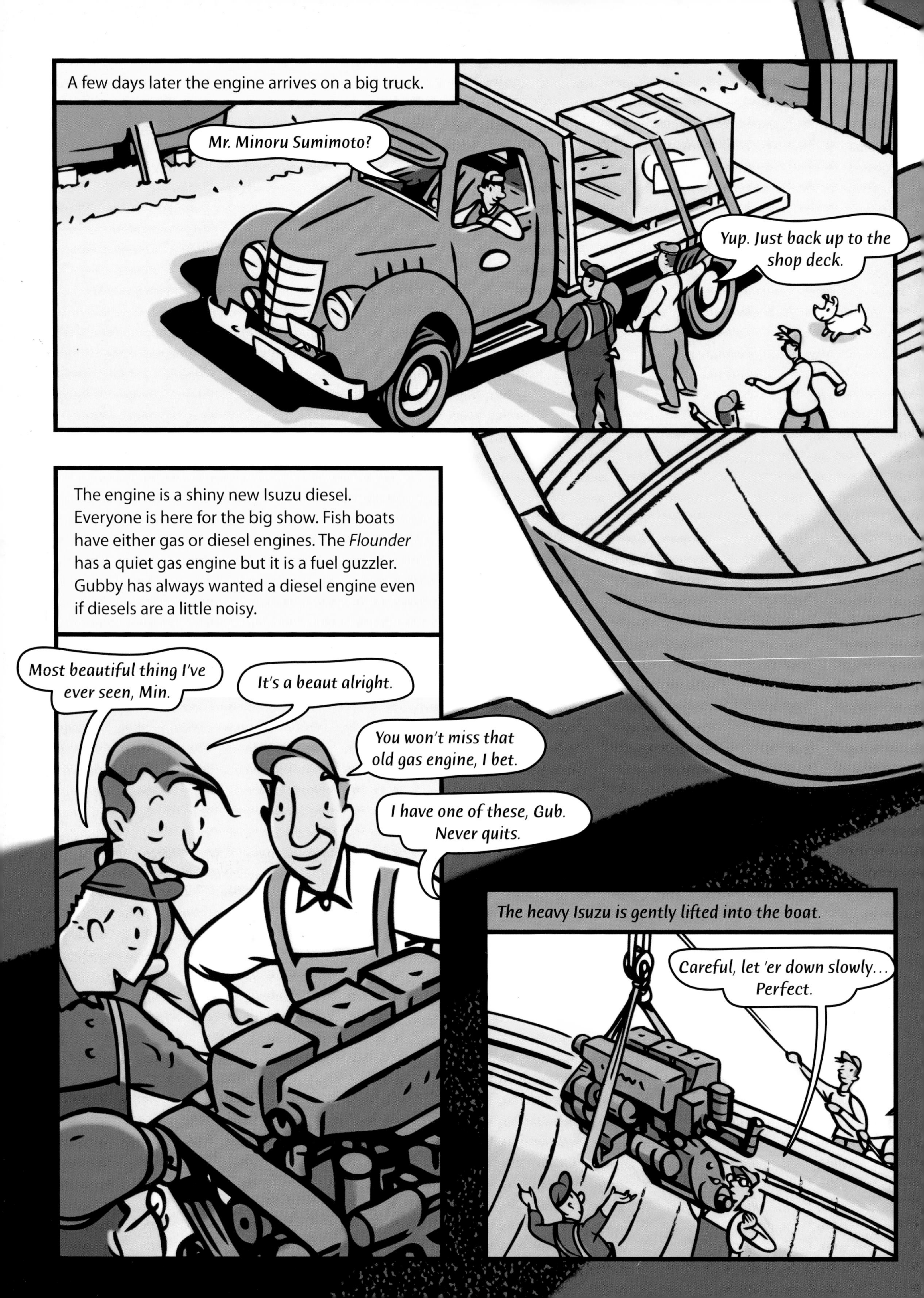
A few days later the engine arrives on a big truck.
Mr. Minoru Sumimoto?
Yup. Just back up to the shop deck.
The engine is a shiny new Isuzu diesel. Everyone is here for the big show. Fish boats have either gas or diesel engines. The *Flounder* has a quiet gas engine but it is a fuel guzzler. Gubby has always wanted a diesel engine even if diesels are a little noisy.
Most beautiful thing I've ever seen, Min.
It's a beaut alright.
You won't miss that old gas engine, I bet.
I have one of these, Gub. Never quits.
The heavy Isuzu is gently lifted into the boat.
Careful, let 'er down slowly… Perfect.

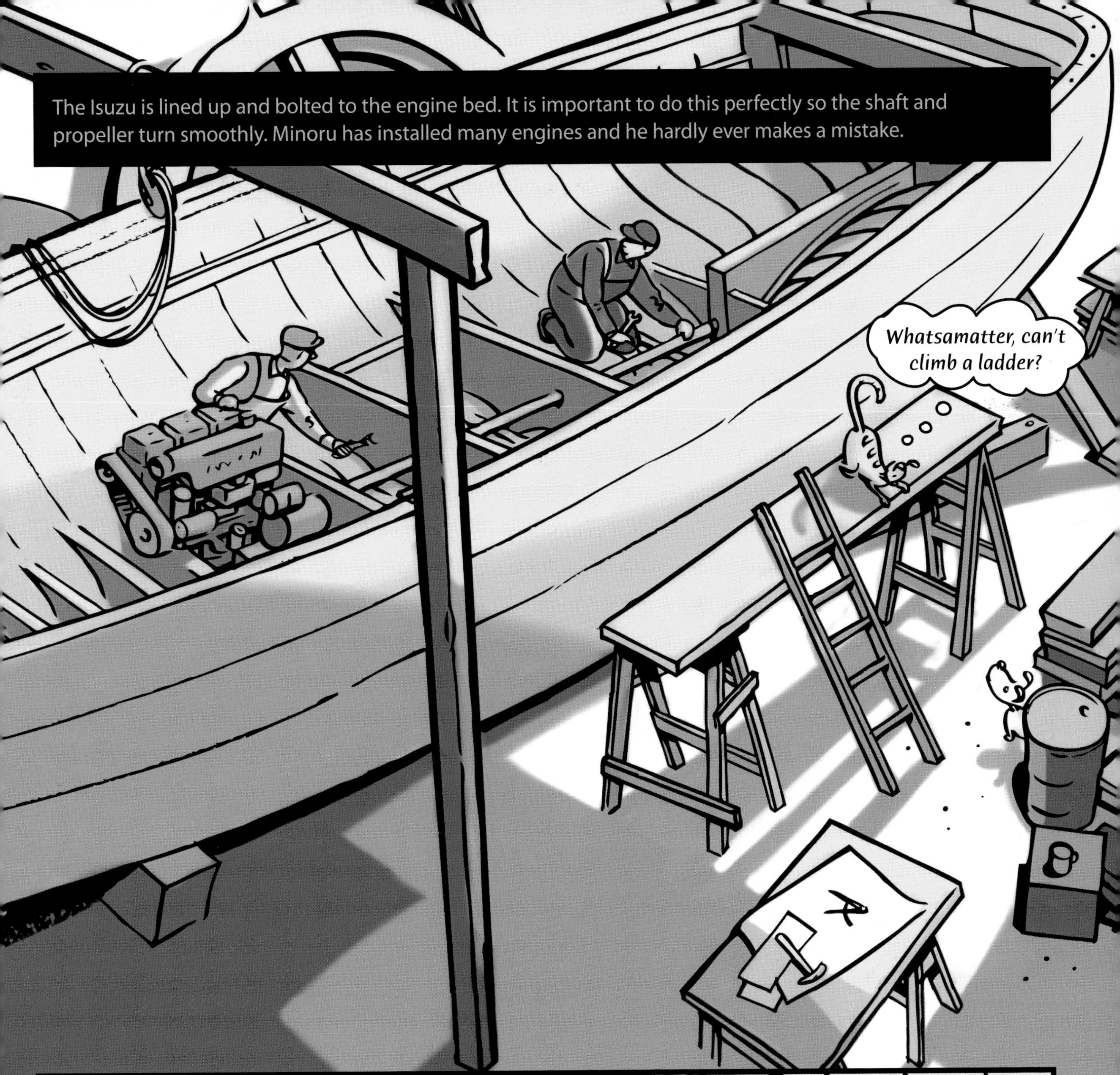
The Isuzu is lined up and bolted to the engine bed. It is important to do this perfectly so the shaft and propeller turn smoothly. Minoru has installed many engines and he hardly ever makes a mistake.
Whatsamatter, can't climb a ladder?

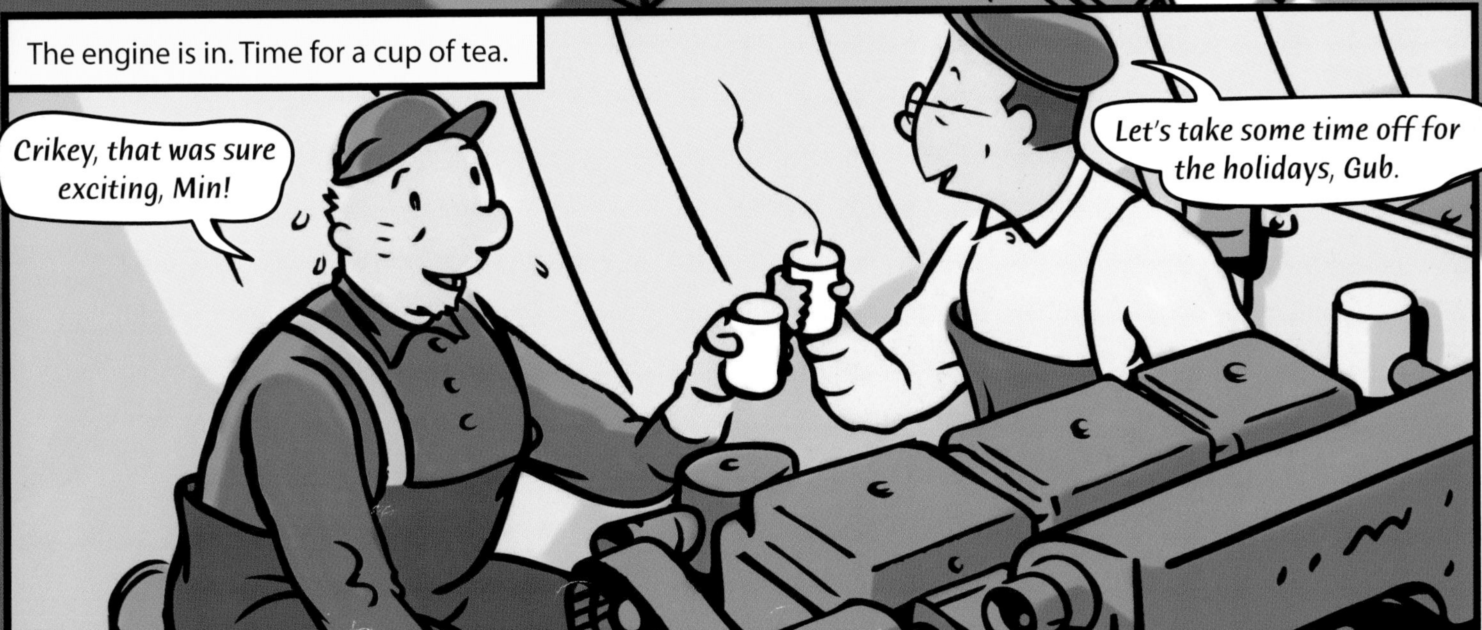
The engine is in. Time for a cup of tea.
Crikey, that was sure exciting, Min!
Let's take some time off for the holidays, Gub.

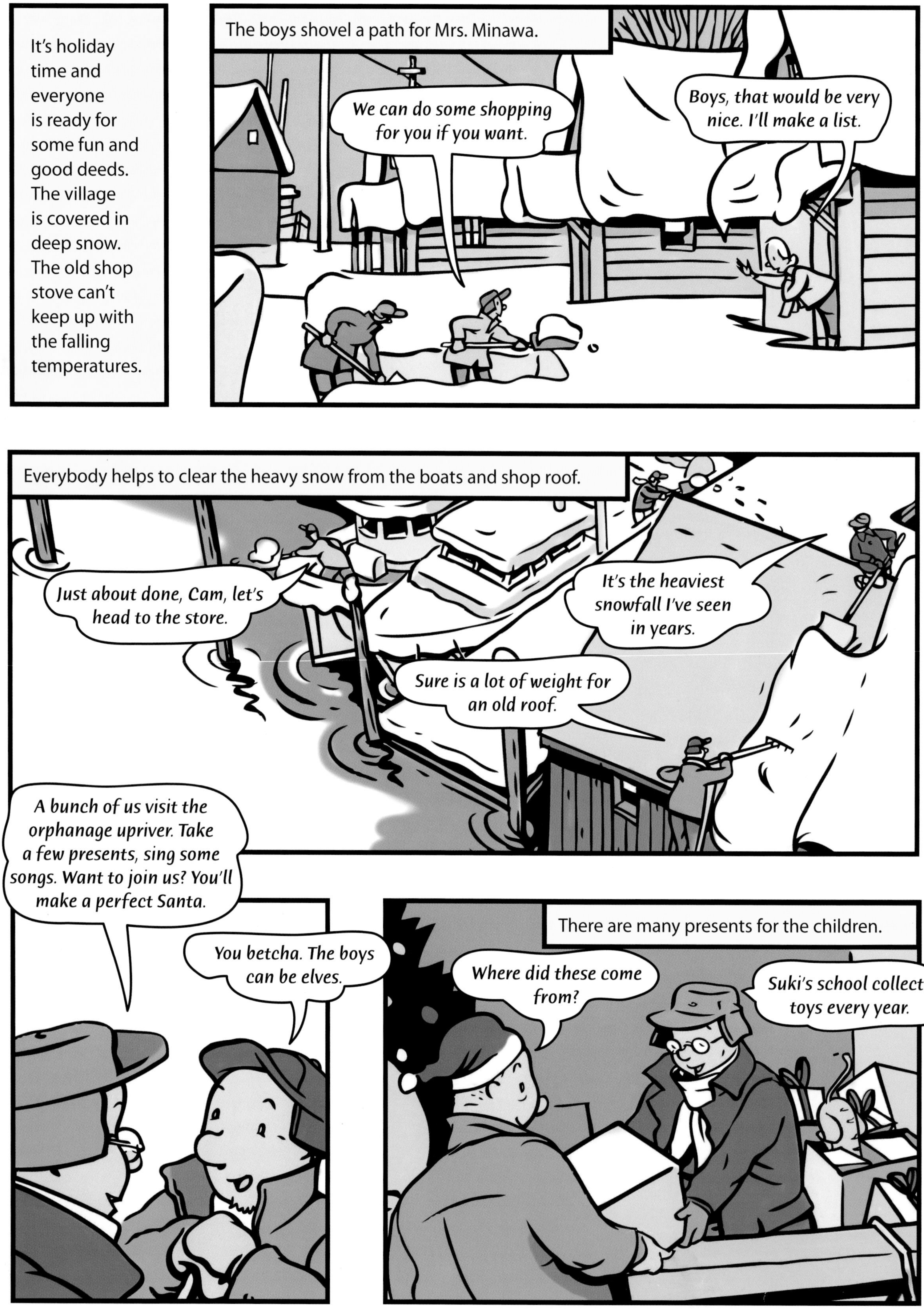
It's holiday time and everyone is ready for some fun and good deeds. The village is covered in deep snow. The old shop stove can't keep up with the falling temperatures.
The boys shovel a path for Mrs. Minawa.
We can do some shopping for you if you want.
Boys, that would be very nice. I'll make a list.
Everybody helps to clear the heavy snow from the boats and shop roof.
Just about done, Cam, let's head to the store.
It's the heaviest snowfall I've seen in years.
Sure is a lot of weight for an old roof.
A bunch of us visit the orphanage upriver. Take a few presents, sing some songs. Want to join us? You'll make a perfect Santa.
You betcha. The boys can be elves.
There are many presents for the children.
Where did these come from?
Suki's school collects toys every year.

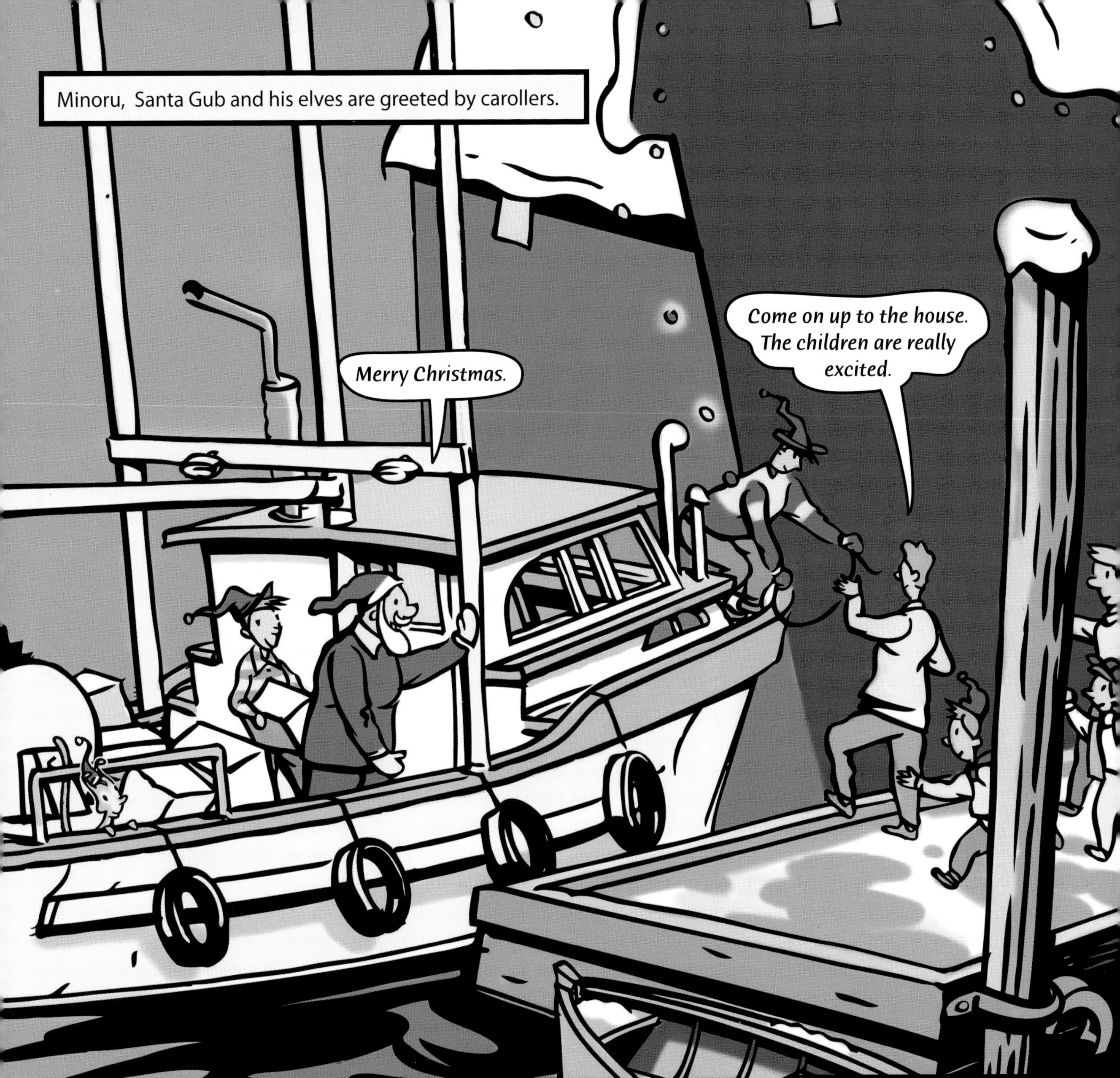
Minoru, Santa Gub and his elves are greeted by carollers.
Merry Christmas.
Come on up to the house. The children are really excited.

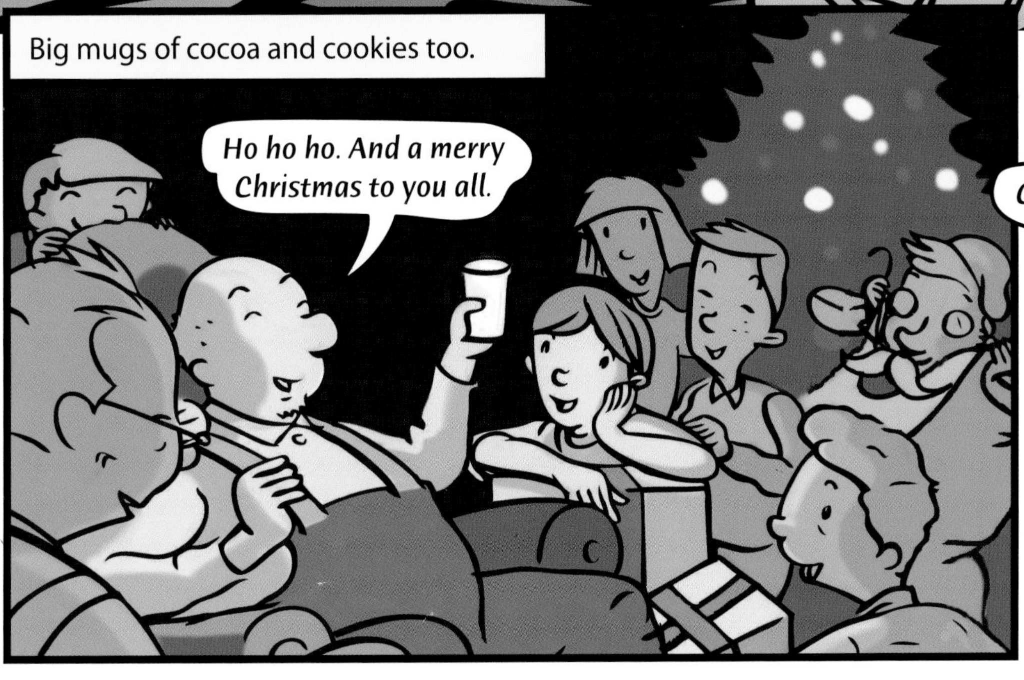
Big mugs of cocoa and cookies too.
Ho ho ho. And a merry Christmas to you all.

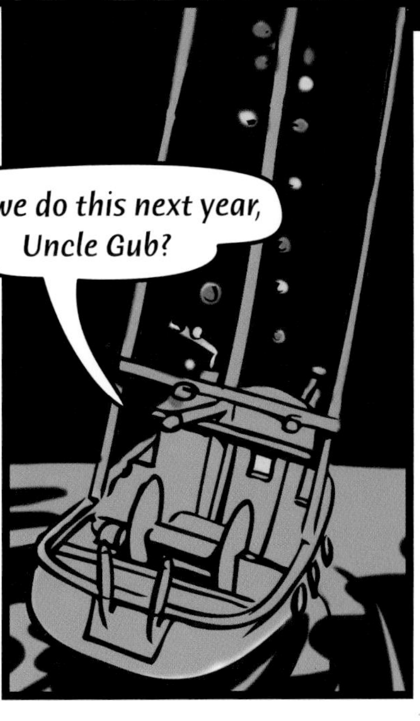
Can we do this next year, Uncle Gub?

The holidays are over and everybody is working on the yellow cedar deck. The deck is very important as it strengthens the hull and must be watertight to protect the crew from stormy seas.

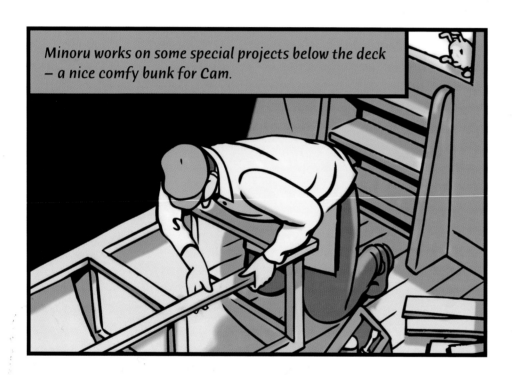

Have a good holiday, Gub?

Musta gained ten pounds from Millie's lemon tarts.

Minoru works on some special projects below the deck – a nice comfy bunk for Cam.

Puss will have his very own bed.

PUSS

Dad has ordered the glass for the windows.

Great! I'll make the door tomorrow.

The wheelhouse is where the boat's steering wheel and cook stove are. Gubby will be living on the boat for many months and he wants it to be really cosy.

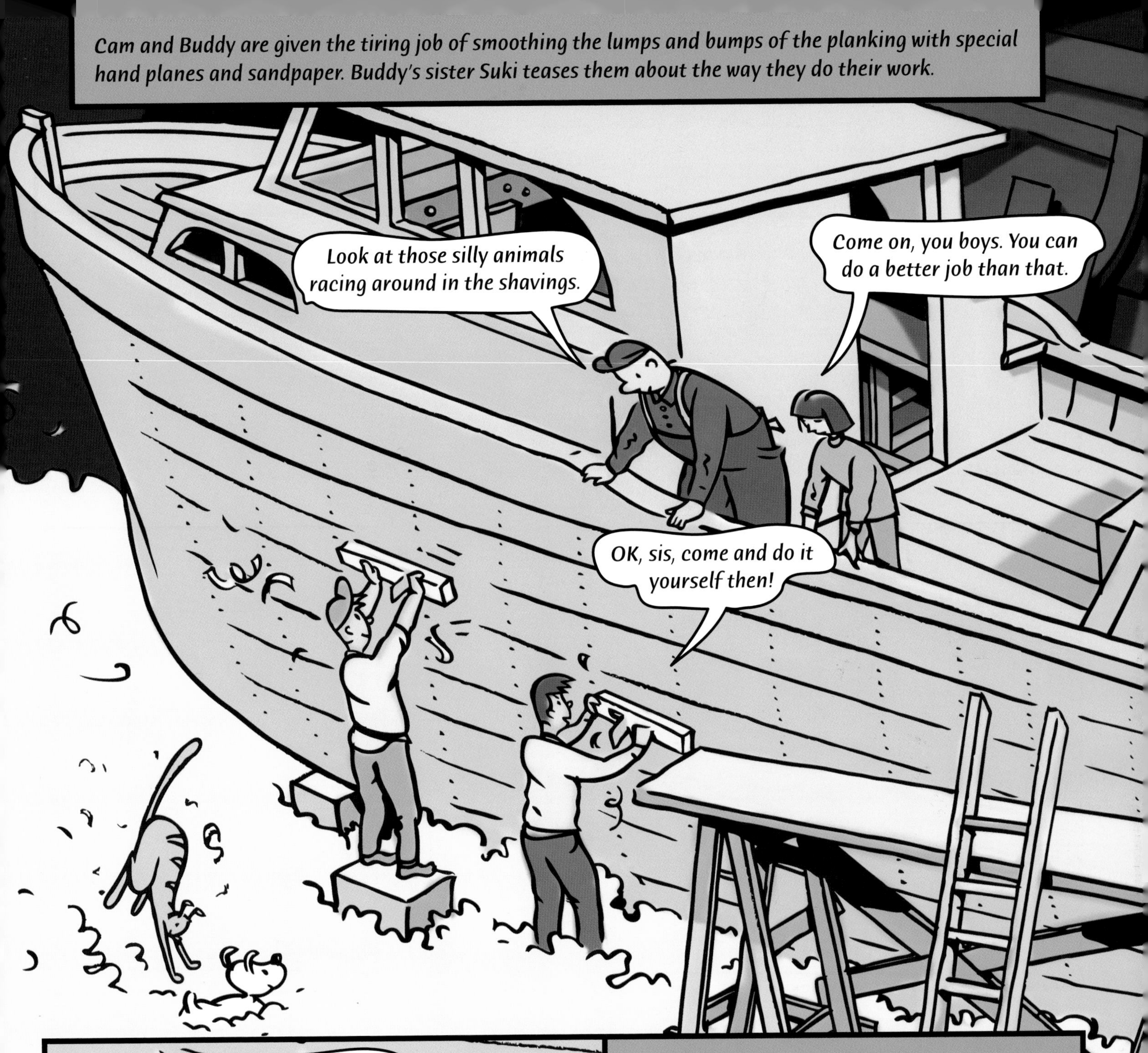
Cam and Buddy are given the tiring job of smoothing the lumps and bumps of the planking with special hand planes and sandpaper. Buddy's sister Suki teases them about the way they do their work.
Look at those silly animals racing around in the shavings.
Come on, you boys. You can do a better job than that.
OK, sis, come and do it yourself then!

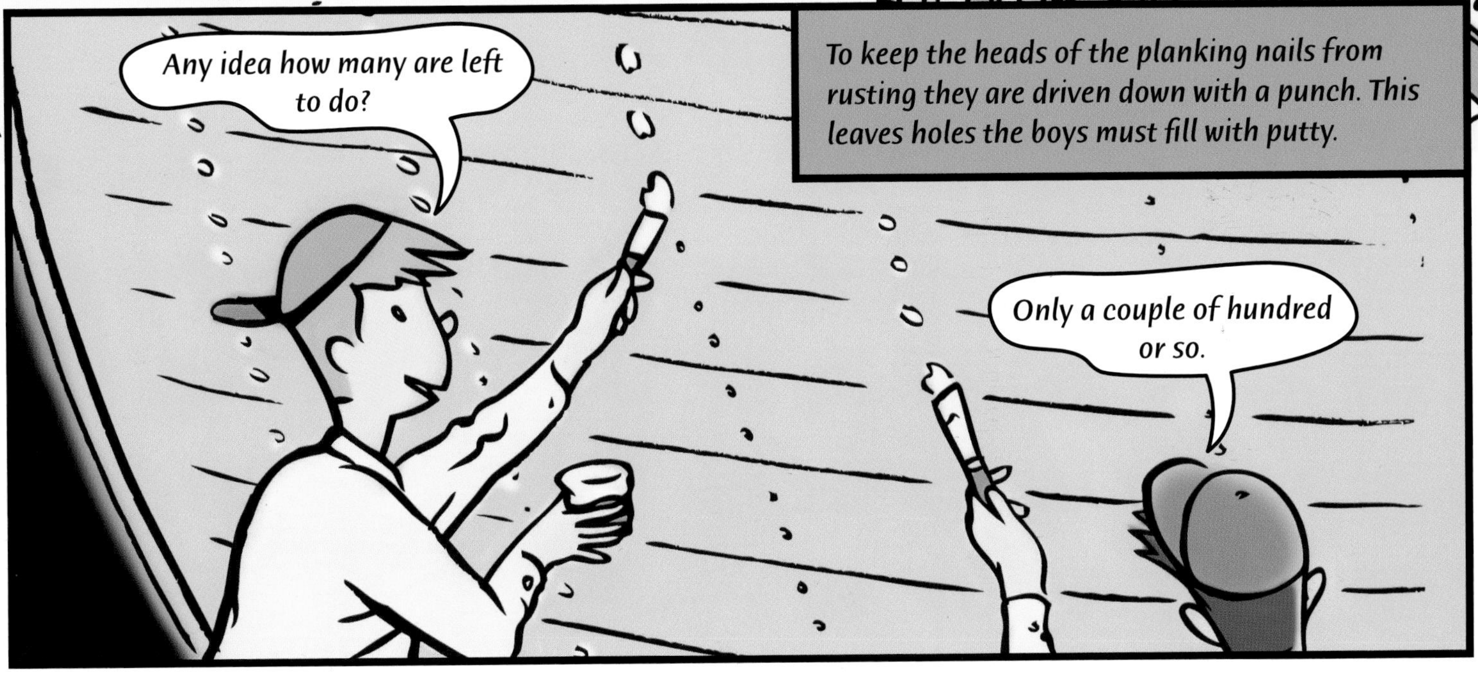
To keep the heads of the planking nails from rusting they are driven down with a punch. This leaves holes the boys must fill with putty.
Any idea how many are left to do?
Only a couple of hundred or so.

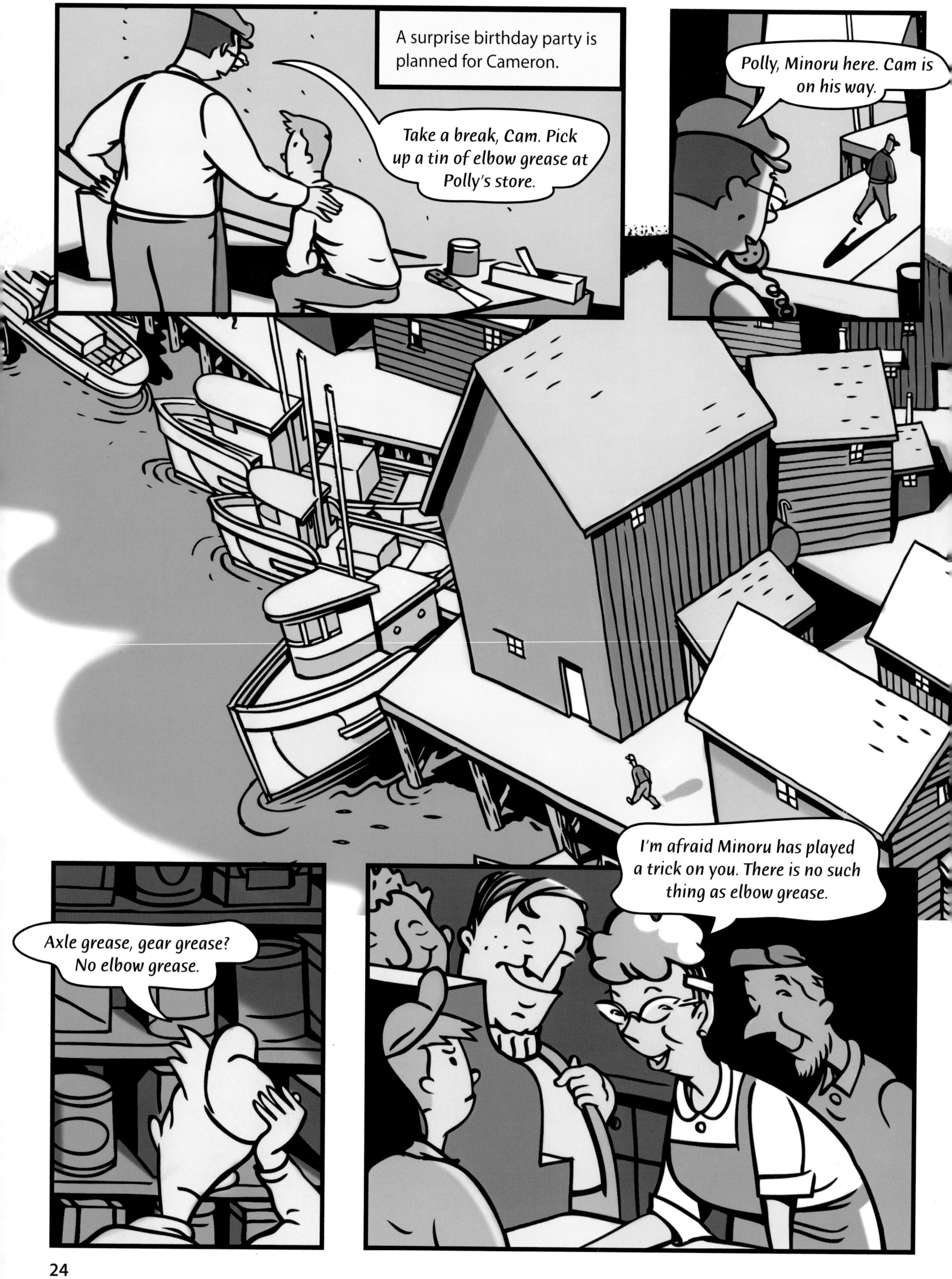
A surprise birthday party is planned for Cameron.
Take a break, Cam. Pick up a tin of elbow grease at Polly's store.
Polly, Minoru here. Cam is on his way.
Axle grease, gear grease? No elbow grease.
I'm afraid Minoru has played a trick on you. There is no such thing as elbow grease.

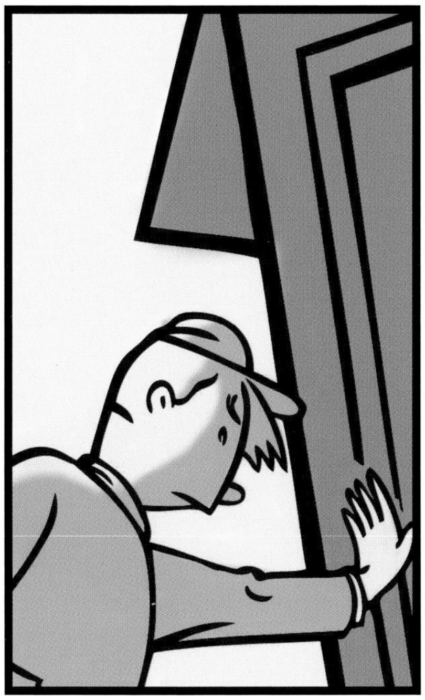

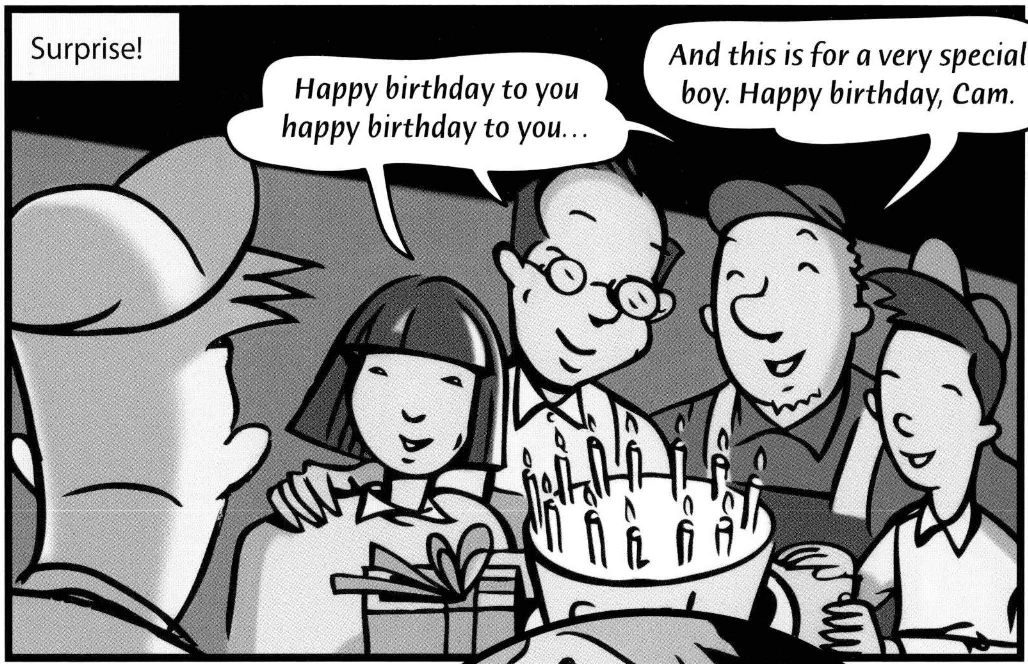
Surprise!
Happy birthday to you happy birthday to you…
And this is for a very special boy. Happy birthday, Cam.

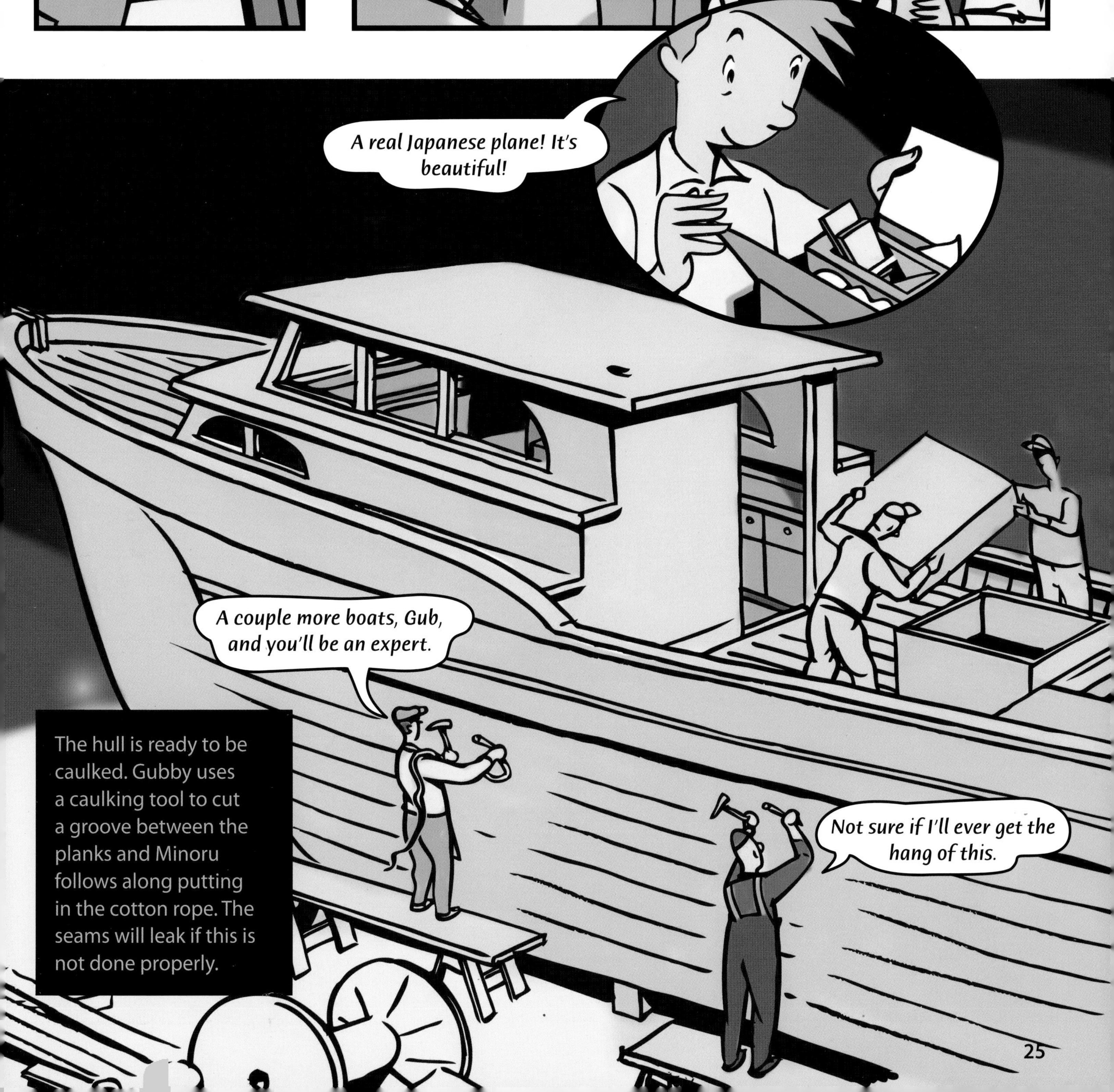
A real Japanese plane! It's beautiful!
A couple more boats, Gub, and you'll be an expert.
The hull is ready to be caulked. Gubby uses a caulking tool to cut a groove between the planks and Minoru follows along putting in the cotton rope. The seams will leak if this is not done properly.
Not sure if I'll ever get the hang of this.

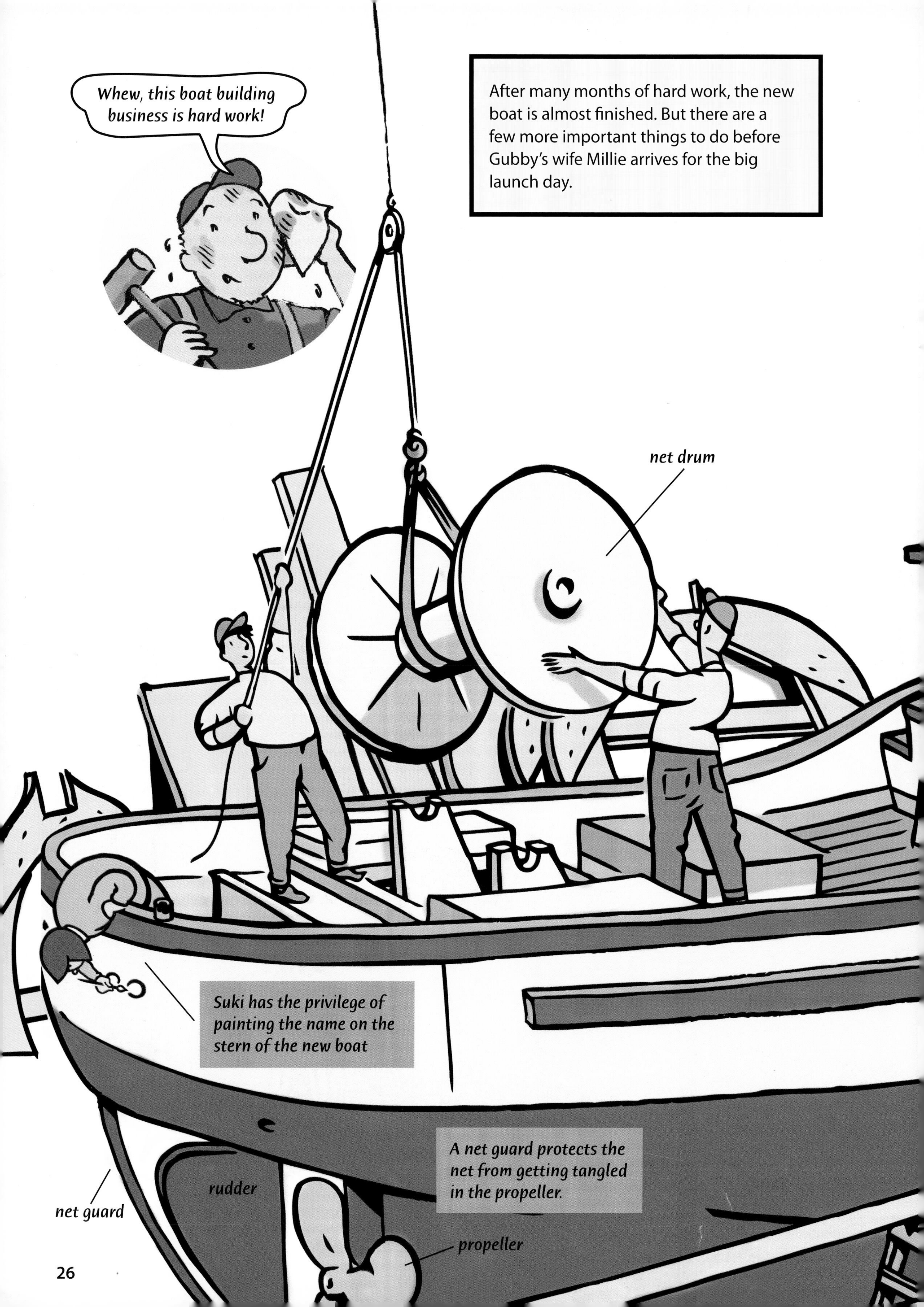
After many months of hard work, the new boat is almost finished. But there are a few more important things to do before Gubby's wife Millie arrives for the big launch day.
Whew, this boat building business is hard work!
net drum
Suki has the privilege of painting the name on the stern of the new boat
A net guard protects the net from getting tangled in the propeller.
rudder
net guard
propeller

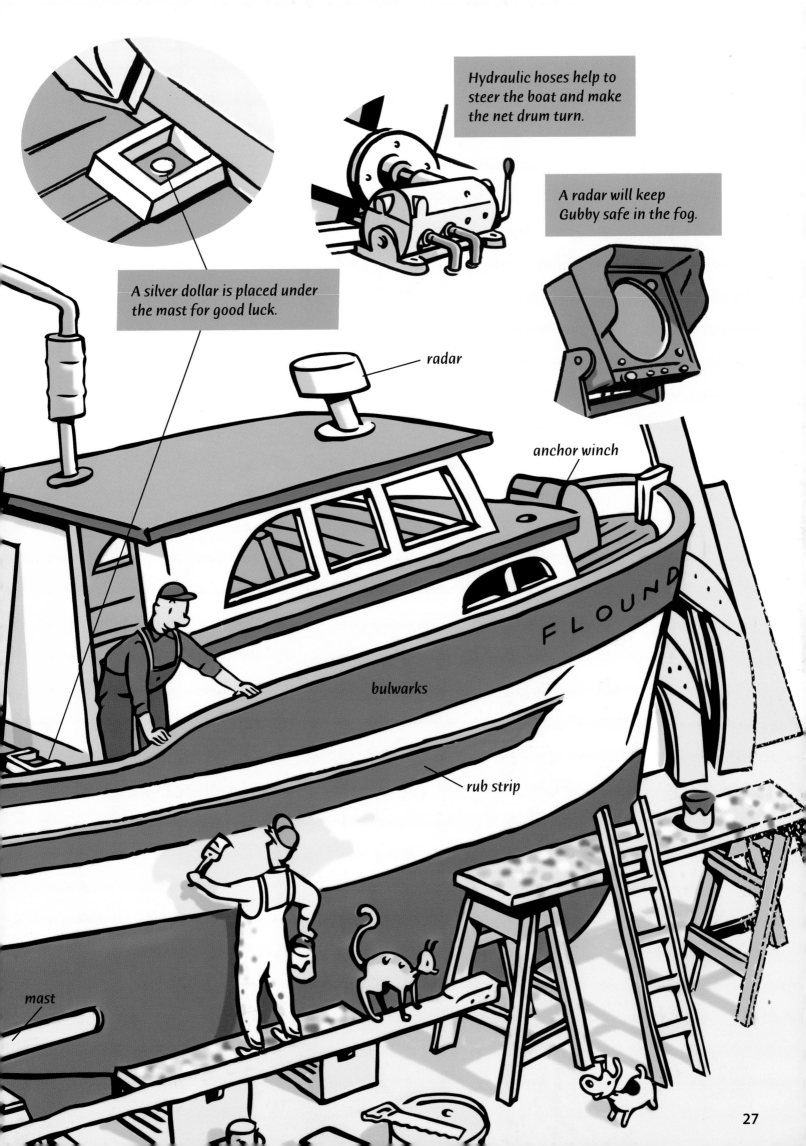

Hydraulic hoses help to steer the boat and make the net drum turn.

A radar will keep Gubby safe in the fog.

A silver dollar is placed under the mast for good luck.

radar

anchor winch

bulwarks

FLOUND

rub strip

mast

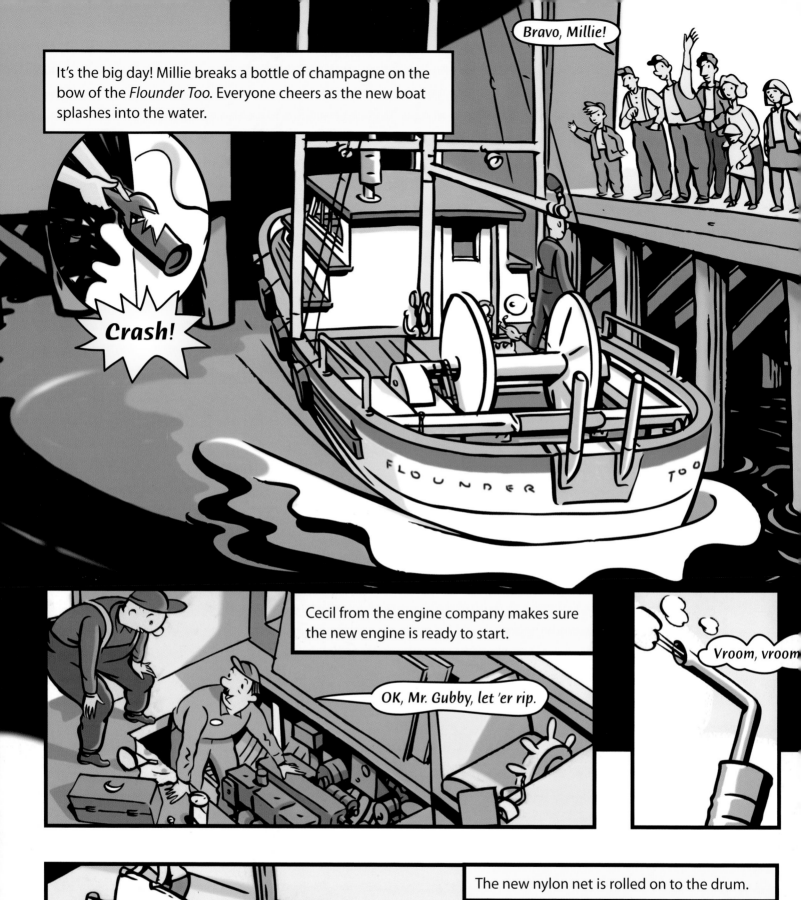

It's the big day! Millie breaks a bottle of champagne on the bow of the *Flounder Too.* Everyone cheers as the new boat splashes into the water.

Bravo, Millie!

Crash!

FLOUNDER TOO

Cecil from the engine company makes sure the new engine is ready to start.

OK, Mr. Gubby, let 'er rip.

Vroom, vroom

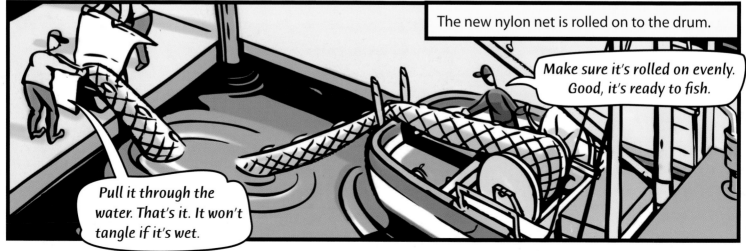

The new nylon net is rolled on to the drum.

Make sure it's rolled on evenly. Good, it's ready to fish.

Pull it through the water. That's it. It won't tangle if it's wet.

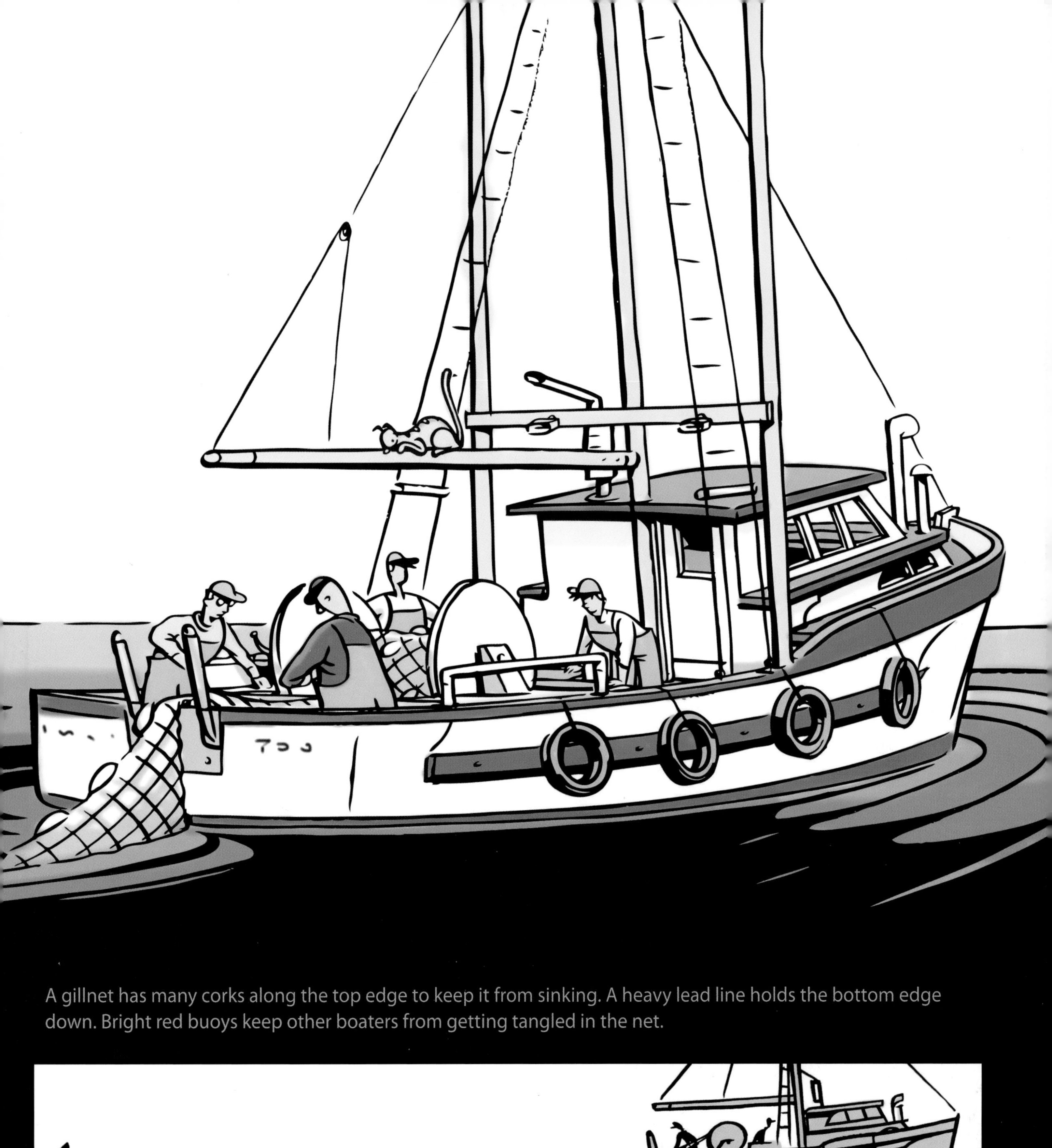

A gillnet has many corks along the top edge to keep it from sinking. A heavy lead line holds the bottom edge down. Bright red buoys keep other boaters from getting tangled in the net.

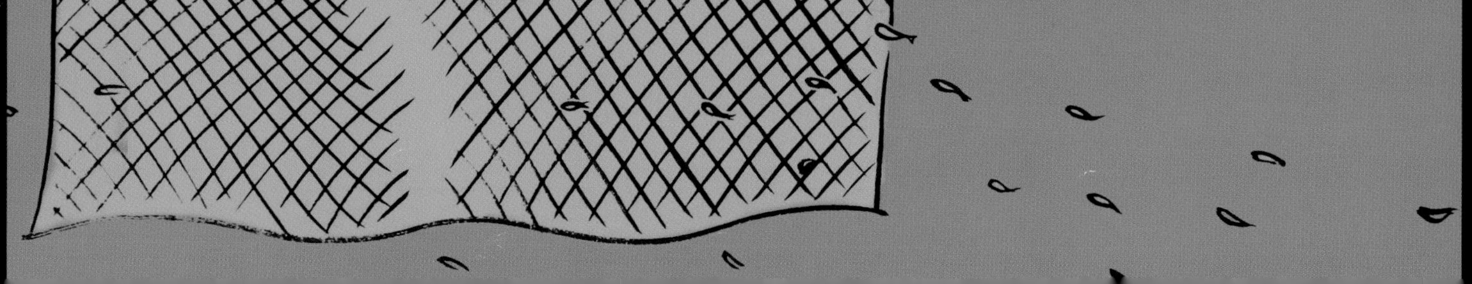

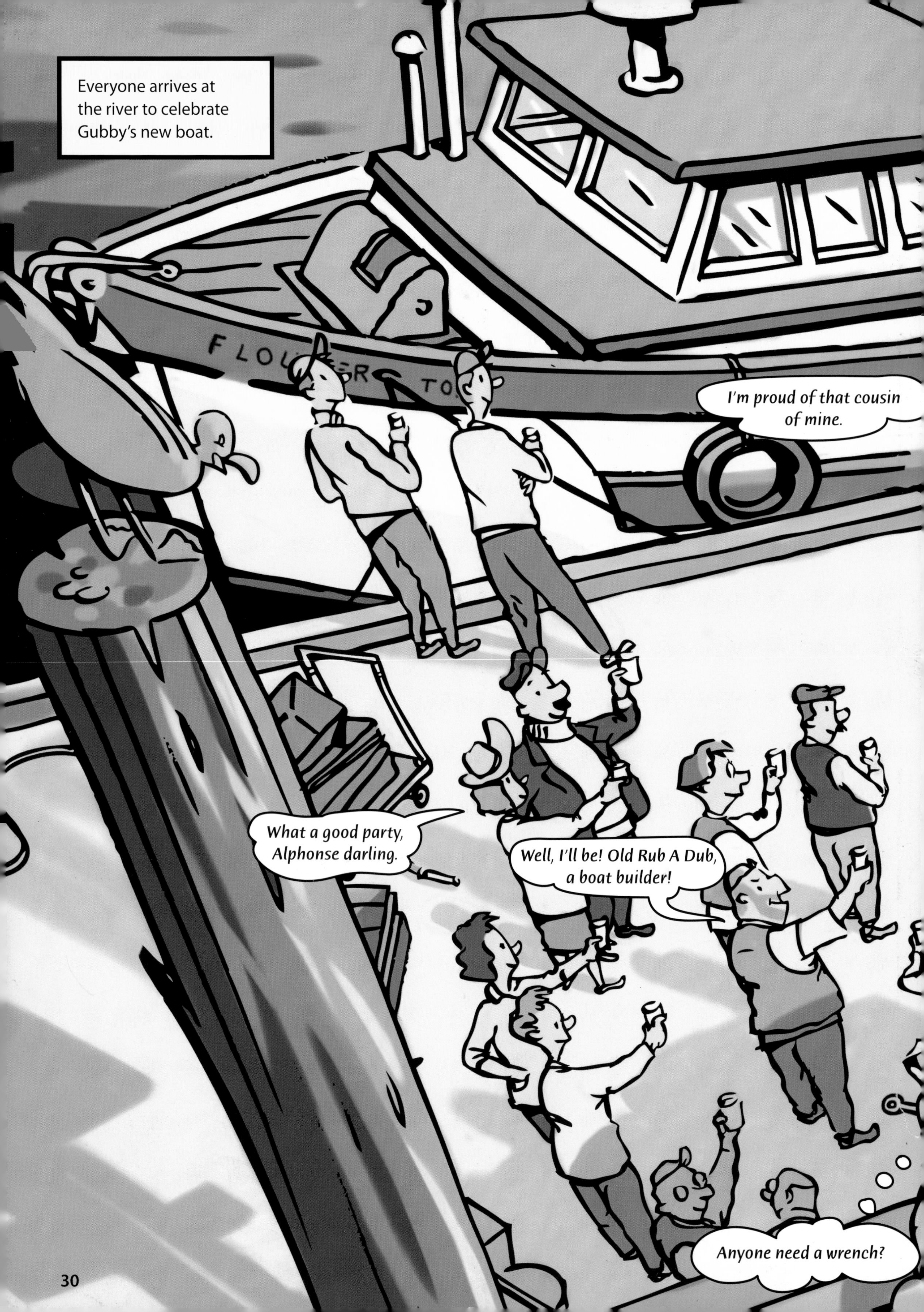
Everyone arrives at the river to celebrate Gubby's new boat.
I'm proud of that cousin of mine.
What a good party, Alphonse darling.
Well, I'll be! Old Rub A Dub, a boat builder!
Anyone need a wrench?

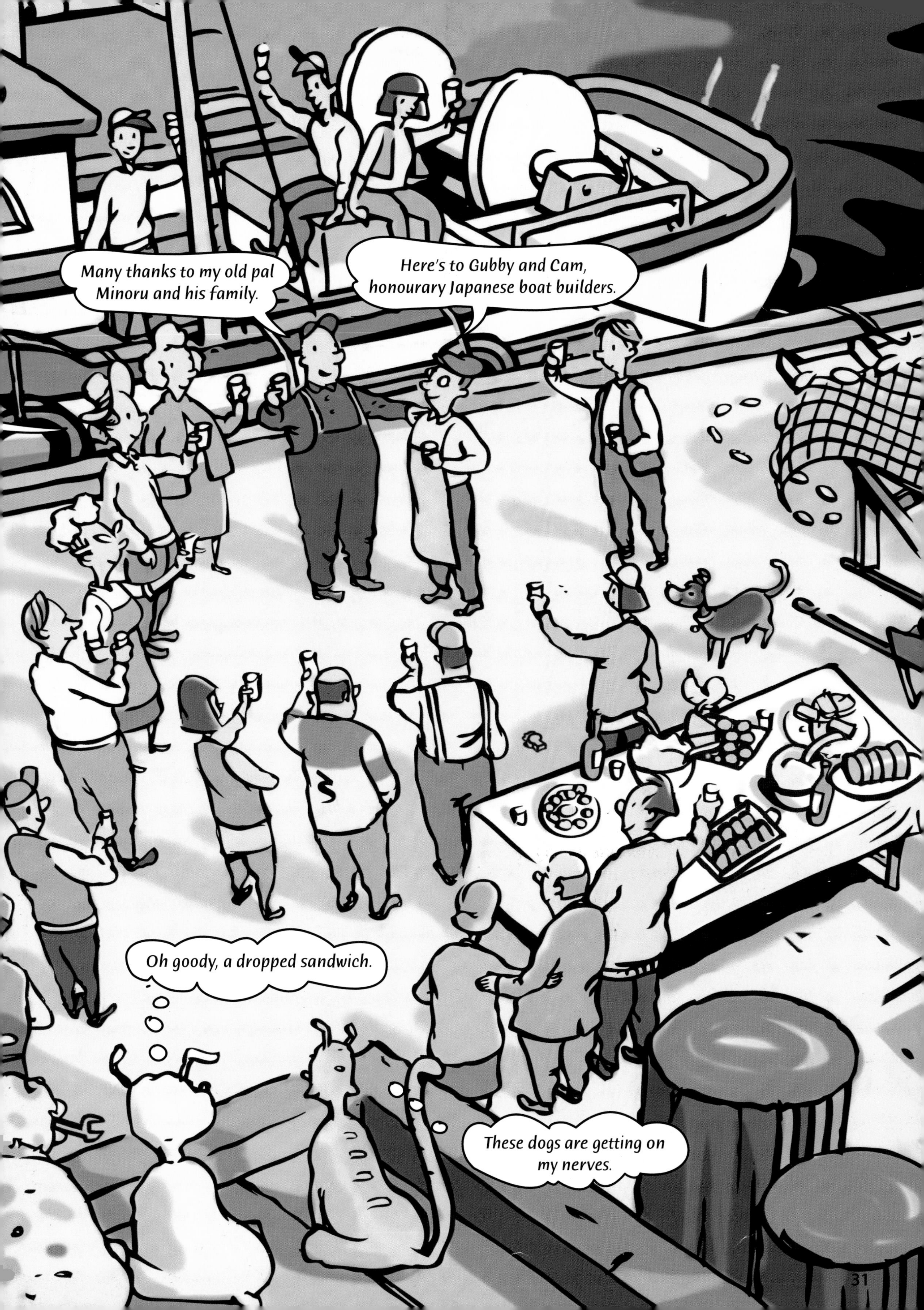
Many thanks to my old pal Minoru and his family.
Here's to Gubby and Cam, honourary Japanese boat builders.
Oh goody, a dropped sandwich.
These dogs are getting on my nerves.

For Buddy
Sakamoto

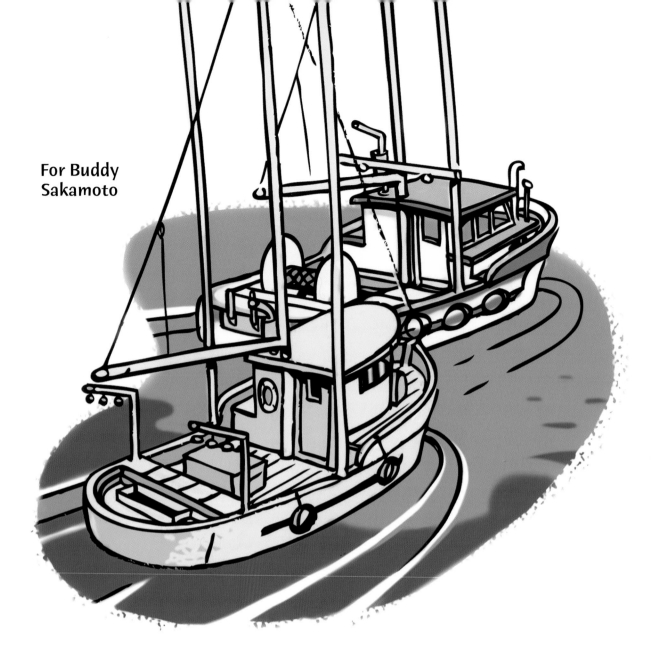

Harbour Publishing Co. Ltd.
P.O. Box 219, Madeira Park, BC, V0N 2H0
www.harbourpublishing.com

Page layout by Kim La Fave. Art direction by Roger Handling, Terra Firma Digital Arts. Printed and bound in Canada. Printed with soy-based ink on chlorine-free paper made with 10% post-consumer waste.

THE CANADA COUNCIL | LE CONSEIL DES ARTS
FOR THE ARTS | DU CANADA
SINCE 1957 | DEPUIS 1957

BRITISH COLUMBIA
ARTS COUNCIL
An agency of the Province of British Columbia

Harbour Publishing acknowledges financial support from the Government of Canada through the Canada Book Fund and the Canada Council for the Arts, and from the Province of British Columbia through the BC Arts Council and the Book Publishing Tax Credit.

Library and Archives Canada Cataloguing in Publication

Kent, Gary, 1941-
    Gubby builds a boat / by Gary Kent ; illustrated by Kim La Fave.

ISBN 978-1-55017-591-2

    I. La Fave, Kim II. Title.

PS8621.E643G83 2012   jC813'.6   C2012-904299-4

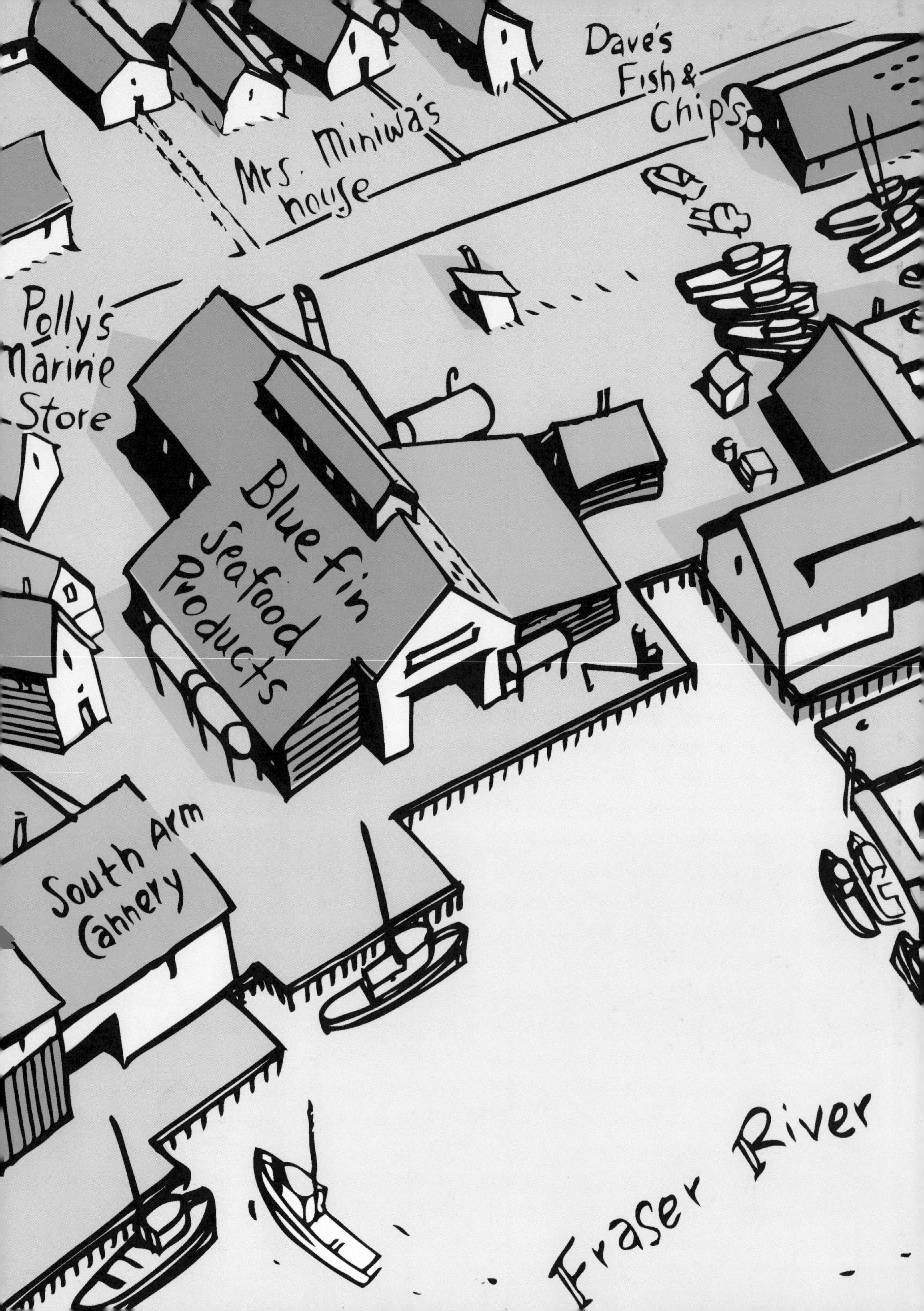
Dave's Fish & Chips
Mrs. Miniwa's house
Polly's Marine Store
Bluefin Seafood Products
South Arm Cannery
Fraser River